THE
STUBBORN
BREED

THE
STUBBORN
BREED

GILES A. LUTZ

DOUBLEDAY & COMPANY, INC.

GARDEN CITY, NEW YORK

1975

JH

ISBN: 0-385-11239-4
Library of Congress Catalog Card Number 75-12225
Copyright © 1975 by Giles A. Lutz
All Rights Reserved
Printed in the United States of America
First Edition

THE
STUBBORN
BREED

CHAPTER ONE

Lou Manard sat astride Dandy, his eyes withdrawn as he watched people stream into the schoolhouse. He listened to the murmur of talk and the bursts of laughter as people greeted each other. He used to look forward to these occasions; the pie and box suppers, or a dance. Such a date was something to fix in his mind, and each passing day, anticipation whittled away at the drab monotony of the never ending procession of farm chores. But that was before Celia Daniels had gone to work for Storhmier.

Lou tried to curb the impatience that swept over him. He should be at Storhmier's tonight, listening to Celia playing the piano and adoring her with his eyes. He had first seen Celia two weeks ago, and it was hard to believe that just seeing another could so change a person's life.

Lou's irritation mounted. Why had he promised the Nalleys over a month ago he would attend this affair? For the past week, he had debated upon telling the Nalleys bluntly that something had happened to change his mind, but each time, he wavered against the final act of refusal. The Nalleys were good people, and he was grateful to them for so many things. Besides, a promise was a promise, even in a simple matter. Lou could salvage something out of this evening; that was why he insisted upon coming here by himself. After the pie supper was over, Lou intended to break away from the Nalleys. Then the rest of the evening would be his to spend at Storhmier's.

The stallion snorted restlessly and repeatedly bobbed his head. Dandy never liked to stand long in one spot. This horse had a lot of stamina, and that eight-mile trip to town hadn't even begun to drain him.

Lou sawed on the reins to quiet the stallion's restlessness. "Whoa, you hammerhead. We just got here." The sternness of his voice didn't disguise the affection he felt for this horse.

Lou had been in the stall when the knobby-kneed colt was dropped. He had watched it struggle to its feet, fighting its ungainly legs to hold his balance. The colt fell four times before he found the mare's teat. Lou's heart swelled with joy; this small one had tremendous determination.

"If you ain't a dandy," he murmured. Those first few moments had named the stallion.

Lou watched those awkward stumbling legs lengthen and strengthen. From the start, he knew this colt was going to grow into something outstanding. Dandy hadn't disappointed him in any way. He had grown into a strapping animal, standing seventeen and a half hands high. Why shouldn't Lou's heart swell with pride? He had a horse other men wanted, for he had seen the way men looked at Dandy. He had turned down more offers to buy Dandy than he could remember.

He jerked on the reins again. "Stop it, Dandy. I'll be the one to say when we leave."

Lou scanned the vehicles in the schoolyard; an odd assortment of wagons and buggies. The Nalleys' buggy wasn't among them, and Lou's heart bounded with the hope that the Nalleys weren't coming. He had refused their offer to stop by and pick him up. Again, he wished there was some way to break his promise without injuring their feelings.

Lou shook his head in resignation, but the faint hope still remained. If the Nalleys didn't show up, he would head for Storhmier's just as fast as he could get there.

He sat there, thinking of Celia Daniels, reveling in the sheer pleasure of his mental picture of her. He would never forget the first night he had seen her. He had stopped in at Storhmier's for a beer and wound up spending the whole evening there. Celia was the sole attraction. How well he recalled the hollow in his stomach as he watched her. He liked everything about Celia Daniels, particularly those big blue eyes in that beautifully formed face. He liked the cant of her head when she looked up at him and the soft peal of her laughter when he said something that amused her. Oh, he guessed he had it bad, but as yet he hadn't said a serious word to her, but he knew he was going to. It was only a matter of picking the right moment. But picking that moment had cost him some sleepless hours. Lou foresaw some rough competition ahead. First, there was her work, for it was easy to see how much she enjoyed it. Against that, Lou could only offer her a life on a farm. He was scared when he thought that such an offer might make her laugh scornfully. But maybe not, he argued with himself. Every time he came in, Celia's eyes would light up with interest as she saw him. Then there was Phil Herrick, Storhmier's bouncer and floorman, to contend with. Herrick was just as interested in Celia as Lou was, for too many times Lou noticed Herrick studying him. Herrick had superior size, but that was the least of Lou's concern about Herrick. What did Herrick have to offer Celia? Surely, a floorman couldn't be making a lot of money. Neither did Lou, but he could offer her land and the prospects of a future. Most importantly, he could offer her security, and that should appeal to any woman.

Dandy bobbed his head again, and the gesture said as plainly as any words, "Make up your mind. Do we stay or go?"

The bobbing head almost made Lou chuckle. He swore that horse could read his mind. He looked around again impatiently. The Nalleys' buggy wasn't in sight. The hope returned stronger than ever; something had happened to keep the Nalleys from coming.

Lou vowed this was the last time he would ever be caught in such a fix. He wasn't engaged to Maude Nalley, in fact, nothing of such serious nature had ever touched his mind. Oh, he liked her well enough, and in the past year he had been seeing her. He had just fallen into a habit, and it was comfortable enough. Maude and Lou had been seen together often enough; so often that the community took it for granted that they were serious about each other.

Lou groaned at being caught in such a drift. At the time he started seeing Maude he could see no harm in their association, but now the drift had spread until Lou felt as though he was caught in a relentless tide. He didn't want to hurt Maude Nalley or her parents. All three were fine people, but none of them was Celia Daniels.

Why was he sitting here, tormenting himself? He could leave now and make his apology to the Nalleys at a later date. None of them had a chain on him.

"Dandy, I guess you're right," he muttered. "I shouldn't have come here in the first place."

The stallion bobbed his head and flicked his ears as though he agreed with every word.

Lou's decision to leave came too late. Before he could turn Dandy, the Nalleys' buggy pulled into the schoolyard. Nalley drove in beside Dandy, and his big voice boomed out.

"Did we keep you waiting, Lou?" he asked.

"No," Lou answered. "I just got here." He avoided looking at Maude. He couldn't stop the guilt he felt.

He swung down and tied Dandy to a hitch rail. Nalley tied up his mare and helped Sarah and Maude down. He lifted a hamper out of the buggy and winked at Lou. "Big evening," he said. "I swear Maude outdid herself tonight."

"Sure," Lou answered woodenly. Maude was an excellent cook. Lou had eaten many a meal at the Nalleys' place.

Nalley and his wife walked a few paces ahead, as they started toward the schoolhouse. Damn it, Lou thought. They're still at it, taking advantage of every opportunity to pair me off with Maude. Lou had nothing against Maude, except that he couldn't remember a time when she hadn't been around. She had tagged him all during their school days, and he could recall too many times he had roughly ordered her to leave him alone. Each time her face would go white at the rebuke, but she was always back the next day. He should have remembered all those times when he thought of her as a nuisance before he started seeing her again.

Lou walked beside Maude, his head lowered. He wasn't a tall man, five foot eight, perhaps a fraction more would catch him. Hard work had pared away any extra flesh. His brown eyes had a weighing quality, at times appearing almost black. The mouth was big over a hard, resolute chin. The sobriety of his expression changed when he was amused. When he laughed, he would throw back his head, displaying strong, even white teeth. He wouldn't call himself the handsomest man in the community, but he didn't think he was the ugliest, either.

Lou lost his mother when he was ten, and Lou felt the loss keenly. He and his father were never close. Doyle Manard had always been a withdrawn, impatient man. He grew worse after his wife's death, yelling at his son when something didn't go to suit him. The Manards owned the only cattle ranch for miles around, and by the usual standards, it was a small one, comprised of only two thousand acres. Lou had grown up seeing the inexorable change in the country. Kansas wasn't cattle country, compared to the states farther west. Kansas was farming land, and soon the Manard operation would be squeezed out, too.

Lou was eighteen years old when he approached his father with news he knew would startle and enrage Doyle.

"Pa, I'm leaving," he announced abruptly. He had to say it fast, or the hollow in his stomach would rise and turn his voice into a squeak.

Doyle looked up from his desk with its clutter of papers. There wasn't much resemblance between father and son. Doyle was blocky and even shorter than his son. Those bushy eyebrows rose as he frowned at Lou.

"What did you say?" he asked absently. His mind was too filled with other things to comprehend what Lou said.

Lou had interrupted his father at a bad time, but it was always that way. Doyle was adding up another batch of bills, trying to squeeze out a profit after the awesome total of expenses was met. As far back as Lou could remember, Doyle fought those bills, usually with the same unhappy results.

"I said I'm leaving, Pa," Lou answered quietly.

"All right," Doyle said impatiently, his attention already turning back to his paper work. "Be back here by noon. I want those cows in the south pasture moved before night. I noticed this morning the grass is getting thin there." That faint note of accusation was back in his voice as though somehow he blamed Lou.

Here was an out; Lou could seize it and run and never bring up the subject again. Lou drew a deep breath. For the past two years he had thought of nothing but striking out on his own. A dozen times he had tried to tell his father, but that damned hollow in his belly had swallowed up his voice. It was now or never.

"I'm leaving for good, Pa." That didn't come out as positive as Lou wanted, but he meant every word. Inwardly, he flinched. Now, hell would rise up and break full in his face.

Doyle's jaw went slack as he stared at Lou. "Did I hear you right?" he asked in an ominous tone.

"You did," Lou said doggedly. "Pa, I want to be on my own. I want to plant seed and grow things." Desperation hurried his voice along. "I was never cut out to be a cattleman. Raising cattle in Kansas is a losing business. Every year proves it a little more."

"You want to be a damned farmer?" Doyle asked incredulously. "Now, ain't that sweet?" There was nothing sweet in his voice. His face reddened as he picked up steam. "Too much of your ma's father rubbed off on you. I shouldn't have allowed you to spend so much time with him while you were growing up."

Lou's face remained impassive. What Doyle said was probably true. Hiram Goodman, his maternal grandfather, was a gentle man. He had time to listen to a youngster and explain things to him. Lou guessed his love for growing things came from Hiram. Hiram's death had been a terrible shock to Lou.

"I'm not going to argue about it, Pa," he said wearily. "It's just something I've got to do."

Doyle was in full rage now. Lou knew there was no use trying to explain anything further to him. The lines of communication had never been strong between them.

"Just where in the hell are you going to plant things?" Doyle roared. "Maybe you expect me to turn over some of my grass to you?"

Lou was sweating, but it was all said, and he felt better. "I've got land, Pa. The land Ma left me." That was the two hundred and twenty acres Hiram left her. It was all Lou's, and Doyle couldn't do anything about it. Doyle had once tried to annex those acres to his own holdings, but Lou's mother had shown a remarkable spark of determination. "No, Doyle," she had said firmly. "That land belongs to me. One of these days, I want Lou to have it."

Doyle stared belligerently at Lou. "You think you can make a living there? Why, hell, your tenant hasn't been able to pay his rent."

Lou was well aware of that. But Hastings was a poor farmer and a lazy one at that. "That's all taken care of, Pa," he said evenly. "Hastings is moving out this week."

Doyle's face was stony hard as he turned back to his paper work. "You can do as you damn well please," he said coldly. "But don't come crawling back here when you go broke."

Lou sighed. The last fragile line of communication between them had been shattered. "I didn't intend to, Pa," he said quietly and left the house.

That was six years ago, and they had been tough years. Lou had never worked so hard in his life, but he had put the farm on a paying base. There was even enough margin to take care of the drought loss of last year. Lou didn't regret leaving the home ranch.

"Lou," Mrs. Nalley called back to him, "guess what pies Maude baked for tonight?"

Her question jolted Lou out of his thoughts, and he said, "I haven't the slightest idea."

"Strawberry," she said gaily. "Your favorite pie." Sarah was a plump, little woman with a merry face. Maude hadn't taken after her mother. She was rawboned like her father and was almost as tall as Lou. She was capable at everything she put her hand to. Lou had been in the Nalley house often enough to see that Maude was an immaculate housekeeper, and she was an excellent cook.

"Fine," Lou answered Sarah and tried to put honest feeling into the word.

He glanced at Maude. Her face was stiff, and she stared straight ahead. Something had happened to upset her, and Lou wondered uneasily what it was.

Lou didn't want to hurt Maude, but there was no way there could be anything between them. Compared to Celia, Maude was a plain woman, but she did have magnificent eyes. They were big and brown, filled with the shining expectancy of a child. Her frequent smiles transformed her face until she was almost pretty. She was a giving woman, filled with warmth and compassion. She had untiring energy, and Lou doubted she ever looked often on the black side. Oh Lord, he thought miserably, she had so many fine qualities. Maybe it was too bad he could feel nothing for her. He angrily swept the thought out of his mind. It made him feel disloyal. After knowing Celia, there would never be another woman.

Men and women clustered around the Nalleys and Lou the moment they stepped into the schoolhouse. Men shook Lou's hand and whacked him on the back, and the women smiled at him. Everybody seemed happy to see him with Maude again. How those expressions would change, if they knew the thoughts running through Lou's mind. He groaned inwardly. My God, the speculations that would arise. He could just imagine the talk that would follow. People talked best about other people, and that tendency could never be smothered. Male and female tongues would waggle when the news got out that Lou had dropped Maude Nalley in favor of that piano player at Storhmier's.

Lou could be grateful to Nalley though, for Nalley kept plowing ahead, parting the people hemming Lou in. "Hey," Nalley kept saying good-naturedly, "I been on my feet all day. I've got to give them some rest."

That good-natured aggressiveness, plus the bulk to back it up, parted people to give Nalley way.

Nalley kept on going until he reached a table at the far end of the room. He placed the basket he carried on it and asked, "How's this table?"

Lou nodded gratefully. That hemmed-in feeling wouldn't be so bad back here. He looked across the table at Nalley and grinned.

Nalley returned the grin. Nalley was a big, bluff man, a serene humor showing on his face. The years of hard work were in his bowed shoulder and in the big work-hardened hands. Lou had an affection for him that he never felt for his own father. Nalley had sort of taken him over the first year Lou had started farming. Not only was Nalley's help invaluable, he kept Lou from making mistakes. Not that they didn't have their disagreements, some of them heated, for Lou had a stubbornness of his own. He disagreed with Nalley, and when he thought he was right, nothing moved him.

Lou smiled faintly as he remembered their last difference of opinion. "Damnedest hard-headed man I ever knew," Nalley had said hotly. "This is the way it's always been done."

"Maybe," Lou had returned. "But does that mean it has to be the right way?"

Nalley grumbled over Lou's hardheadedness the rest of the morning, but before the day was out, Nalley admitted that Lou was right.

The relationship between them was a good, solid thing, strengthened by their disagreements instead of being weakened. Lou thought the world of Sam Nalley.

Lou sat across from Maude. She still hadn't said anything, and that was unusual. She wasn't a gabby woman, but she wasn't a mouse, either.

"Do you feel all right?" Lou asked.

Maude gave him a full sweep of her eyes before she looked away. "Why shouldn't I?"

Was that a bite in her tone? "I don't know," Lou said lamely. "You're just sort of quiet."

She looked at him again. Lou wouldn't say there was dislike in her eyes, but it wasn't friendliness, either. "Maybe a little tired," she said.

Lou's face heated at the curtness of her tone. Damn it, he wasn't asking her to talk to him.

Sarah pulled the first of the pies out of the basket, babbling incessantly.

Lou watched Maude covertly. If she didn't want to talk to him, that was all right with Lou. Maybe he was being unreasonable, and he tried to change his attitude. He could say one thing for Maude; she hadn't inherited her mother's tongue. He sat there in injured silence, and he supposed it was because Maude made him feel guilty. Damn it, he had never promised her a thing. It wasn't as though he had broken a vow or anything of that sort. He wished to God he hadn't come tonight.

Sarah never stopped talking as she cut the pie. She handed Lou the largest piece, glancing archly at him. For a childish moment, Lou wanted to refuse it. He had the feeling of being dishonest, as though accepting the pie created a bond that put him under obligation.

The sight and smell of the pie got to him, weakening all his stiff-necked resolve. Any resistance he may have felt crumbled as he took his first bite. He closed his eyes in pure bliss, then he looked at Maude and said, "I never tasted better pie." He wasn't trying to make up anything to her; he meant every word.

Maude glanced at him, then looked away. Even his praise couldn't pull a response from her, but Lou didn't miss the faint wave of color stealing into her face. At least, what he said pleased her.

"Maude didn't like the way the crust turned out," Sarah went on. "I told her she didn't have to worry."

Lou cut into his pie again. This was the way pie crust should be, light and flaky. "She didn't," he agreed promptly.

Sarah pressed another piece on Lou, meeting little resistance from him.

"It does me good to see you eat like that," she said, and there was a note of triumph in her voice.

Nalley handed over his plate for another slice. "I want you to keep on feeling good," he said.

Sarah sniffed. "You always eat this way. It's Lou I worry about."

Lou started to wave away the offer of a third slice, then weakened. "About half that much," he said. "I'm making a hog of myself," he confessed.

"It's the highest compliment you could pay Maude," Sarah assured him.

Nalley patted his stomach as he looked at the remains of the second pie. "We made a pretty good hole in it, didn't we?"

"We sure did," Lou replied. His belly was filled, and he should be lazily content, but he wasn't. He wondered how much longer he would have to spend here before he could get away.

"There's a whole pie left," Sarah said. "I'm going to offer it to Mr. and Mrs. Hammer."

"Biggest favor you ever did Claude," Nalley grunted. "I've tasted some of her baking."

"You can carry it over to them, Sam," Sarah said.

"It's not that heavy—" Nalley started.

Sarah cut him short. "Didn't you tell me you wanted to talk to Claude?" she asked sweetly.

Nalley glanced at his wife, then at Maude. "I sure did," he said with false heartiness, and lumbered to his feet. "We'll be right back," he said over his shoulder.

Lou felt a small regret as he watched them go. He had a faint hope the remaining pie would be offered to him to take home. Until tonight he had almost forgotten just how good a cook Maude was. He wanted to compliment her but was afraid she would take it as encouragement. Maybe it was best to remain silent.

Maude looked directly at Lou for the first time.

Lou tried to read her emotions in her eyes, hurt perhaps and certainly anger.

"You don't have to sit here and suffer with me," she said stiffly.

Lou's eyes widened in astonishment. "I didn't say anything like that," he protested.

"You didn't have to," she snapped. "It shows."

Lou's face reddened. This wasn't the Maude he had known during their school days; she had never showed this much spunk before.

Her words sparked his own anger. "You started this," he said heatedly. "I was just sitting here with my thoughts, and you jumped me."

"You go ahead and make a bigger fool of yourself," she said tartly. "I won't try to stop you."

Lou sucked in a ragged breath. That really infuriated him. "What the hell are you talking about?" he demanded roughly.

Her breathing was too rapid, making her words jerky. "Don't you think everybody knows what you've been doing?"

"Ah," Lou said. His face was cold and hard. He wasn't going to admit anything yet, but she knew about Celia. He could depend upon some waggling tongue to be sure to get the news to her.

"Maybe you'd be happier if I left," he said.

She shrugged. "Suit yourself."

Lou shoved away from the table and stood. This was a new Maude, one he had never seen before. He seethed inwardly and paused long enough to say with a sarcastic bite, "I enjoyed the pie. I wish I could say the same about everything else."

He tried to stare Maude down and failed. Her eyes wouldn't budge a fraction. What in the hell had put this tough streak in her? He whirled and strode away from the table. If he didn't get some fresh air, he would choke.

CHAPTER TWO

Lou's neck burned as he plunged through the people in the room. His abrupt departure would elevate more eyebrows, for if people hadn't heard the quarrel with Maude, surely they couldn't have missed seeing what happened. Lou hadn't been too careful about keeping his voice down. The normal hum of talk in the room was momentarily stilled. Oh God, how it would break out the moment he left. Lou wouldn't have had that quarrel happen with Maude for anything in the world, but he wasn't taking the entire blame. He was just sitting there wrapped in his own thoughts, and Maude had jumped all over him. His sorrow that it happened wasn't enough to wipe out the relief it gave him. That should end everything Maude thought was between them.

Lou hurried out of the door and headed for Dandy. He would have to make his apology to Sam and Sarah Nalley later. If this didn't put a breach between him and Nalley, nothing would.

A half-dozen men were gathered just outside the building, and Lou wanted to avoid them. They didn't know what happened back there, but still Lou didn't want to talk to them.

"Hey, Lou," a voice called. "Come over here."

Lou groaned. He knew every one of those men, and he considered them friends. There was no sense in offending them. Lou didn't want the entire community down on him.

Unwillingly he slackened his stride and turned toward them.

Westhoff was the man who called to Lou, and he slapped Lou on the shoulder. "Everything going your way, Lou?"

Lou glanced sharply at him, picking at something devious in the words. If Maude had heard about Celia, surely Westhoff had. He saw nothing sly in Westhoff's face. Westhoff meant just what he said and no more.

"About as good as I could hope for," Lou said flatly.

"Did you eat too much?" Mellinger asked. "I know I did. I envied you."

"Why?" Lou couldn't keep the tension out of his voice. What did Mellinger mean by that?

"Eating the pies Maude made," Mellinger replied easily. "I had to eat the pie my old lady baked." He grimaced. "I wasn't as lucky as you."

The tension slipped away from Lou, and he forced a stiff grin. That exchange with Maude made him suspicious of anything others might say. "Maude's a good cook," he said evenly.

There wasn't a single dissenting word, and Lou relaxed and felt more at ease. These were his friends; they weren't out here to pick or jeer at him. Thank God, not one of them said a word about Celia, even actually or by implication. Maybe men kept a tighter rein on their tongues than women. Lou amended that. In all fairness, these men didn't have the reasons driving Maude.

There were physical differences between these men; some were short, others fat, but the same stamp of the soil was on every one of them. Their hands were gnarled and stained from handling the earth, and that made a common brotherhood. They knew the hopes that rose so high in the spring and the crushing defeats that came afterward. A farmer was a resilient animal, Lou thought. No matter how often he was crushed, he always sprang up again. Lou knew and felt a common bond with these men. Nature was an unmitigated bitch. She slapped a man in the face repeatedly before she relented. Farming was about as big a gamble as a man could take. He bet his money against the whims of nature, the onslaught of the weather, the never-ending attacks of insects. Added to all that were the vagaries of the market. A man not only put all his money into the gamble, he put in his body and soul as well. He grew a little older each year and that much more weary. No wonder the lines etched deeper into his face.

Every man standing around Lou, if given the chance to change to another line of work, even with a guarantee of more security, would turn it down. They were a unique and stubborn breed of men, Lou thought, and he was proud to be one of them. He was luckier than most farmers, for he owned his land free and clear. He could thank his mother for that, and Hiram too.

"We're going to have a good year," Riley said suddenly.

That aroused jeering comment, and Nabor asked, "You give a guarantee with that promise?"

"My God, don't we deserve one?" Riley asked passionately. "I stood and watched the damned drought take my crops last year. That's dying the slow and hard way. Every day, it grew a little drier. I kept hoping long after I knew there was no more hope. I prayed every night—" He broke off in sudden embarrassment.

All of them nodded solemnly. Riley had no need to feel embarrassed. They had gone through the same thing and prayed for just a little rain.

"Wonder who's bigger," Mellinger mused. "God or the bank?"

That was pure sacrilege. Eyes widened and mouths slackened.

"That's a hell of a question," Eveland muttered. "You better never let the Reverend hear you say such a thing."

He saw Lou's grin, and it angered him. "You think it's funny?"

"Not funny, Gil," Lou said gently. "But I know what Mellinger is trying to say. He was just trying to be humorous. When we get in a hole, who do we turn to? Isn't it always the bank?"

They studied Lou's answer a moment, then heads nodded slowly. Now they understood what Mellinger was trying to say.

"I sure ran to the bank fast enough," Nabor said reflectively. "I wound up the year with nothing except a bigger debt on my place. Another year like the last one, and the bank winds up with everything."

"That's the God's truth," Westhoff said. "That's a damned big boat, big enough to hold all of us."

Lou almost felt a sense of guilt. He wasn't in that boat. Last year had been bad in that he hadn't made any money, but he had been able to tough it through without going into debt.

"How's your corn look, Lou?" Riley asked.

Lou was glad the subject was changed. "Never saw it looking better at this time of year. But I tell you that slight dry spell right after planting scared the hell out of me."

Nobody disagreed with what Lou said. There was never a good time for a drought, but this early one came at a particularly bad time, for the seeds needed moisture to sprout and grow.

Nabor slapped his thigh and cackled at a memory. "I was dressing when I heard that rain. I ran out and danced in it without waiting to put my pants on. The old lady thought I'd gone crazy."

They grinned at Nabor's words, and several spoke of what they had been doing when the rain came.

"We sure got no complaint after that rain," Riley stated. "In three days, the corn was poking its way out of the ground. When we needed another rain, it came. It's proof we don't have to worry about another drought this year."

Lou was unconsciously shaking his head, and Nabor demanded, "You don't agree with that?"

"I wish I could," Lou said seriously. "But it could happen again." At the protest forming in their faces, he said fiercely, "Couldn't it? Have we got a guarantee against it?" He hated to put a damper on their high, good spirits, but he was only being realistic.

Nabor eyed Lou dourly. "Damned if you ain't the prophet of gloom. What are you trying to do? Wish all of us into bankruptcy?"

"You know better than that," Lou replied. "But every one of us knows how unpredictable nature can be."

All of them were set against him; he could see it in their faces. He wasn't trying to put a fear in them; he was only trying to be practical.

"You got a way to beat that?" Nabor asked flatly.

"Maybe," Lou said. "Maybe we'll have to quit planting corn and find a new crop to plant. Maybe this isn't the right country for corn."

"Hell, boys," Mellinger said. "He's got a brand-new idea. What are we going to use to replace corn? Maybe he'll suggest planting money trees." He couldn't hold back his laughter. "Ain't you forgetting something, Lou? Money trees need water, too."

Mellinger's laughter stirred up mirth in the others, and Lou waited patiently for it to die down.

"That's an idea," he said, his grin showing no offense. "I wish we could plant that kind of crop. No, I was thinking of wheat."

That stunned them, and they gaped at Lou. He marshaled his arguments for what he proposed. "I'm talking about red Turkey wheat," he said slowly. "They've been planting it in western Kansas the last couple of years, and it's drier than here. I've been reading reports of what they're doing with it out there. Getting pretty good results."

Tilden snorted. "Give it another year or two, and you'll hear no more about it. Just a new fad. Besides, I'm too old to be learning new tricks. I know how to raise corn."

They were all ready to join Tilden. Lou could read it in their faces. He held up a hand to check them.

"Damn it," he said explosively. "I'm not suggesting we quit planting corn. All I'm saying is that we ought to look into it. Wheat's got several things in its favor." His passion had their attention now, and he drove ahead. "When do we usually get our droughts? In the summer just when corn needs moisture to grow and develop. Wheat's planted in mid-September when the greatest danger of drought is over."

Doubt remained on their faces, but they were listening.

"By planting then, wheat gets a chance to establish its roots before winter sets in," Lou went on. "From what I read, snow helps wheat. It soaks the ground, and wheat takes off in the spring, but best of all, it's harvested before a real drought usually sets in."

He hadn't convinced them, for the dubiousness remained on the faces around him, but some of the facts he pointed out would remain with them.

"I dunno, Lou," Mellinger said. "I'm like Tilden. Too old to start learning all over again." A thought occurred to him, for his face brightened. "Are you going to plant any wheat this fall?"

That was a clinching argument, and Mellinger winked at the others.

"I'm thinking about it," Lou said steadily. "I may put out some and see how it does."

"Then we'll wait and see how it turns out for you," Mellinger said. He cackled in triumph. "You go to school for us."

Lou grinned at the laughter running among them. He felt no rancor toward these men. Every new idea would have its tough going.

"What are you boys arguing about?" Welles Parnell asked. "I could hear you all the way from the door."

Everybody turned to face Parnell. He was a short man with a pompous air. Owning the only bank in town gave Parnell considerable standing. He also had a reputation as a shrewd handler of land. Lou had no idea how many farms Parnell had picked up. He had never cared much for Parnell, though he had to use the only banking facilities the town had. He guessed it was Parnell's aggressive nature to take over everything he touched, and that included any discussions he entered.

"No argument, Welles," Mellinger said. "Just a little discussion. Lou has a wild hair. He was telling us how we could take the gamble out of farming."

Parnell's cold blue eyes swept over Lou. "Is that so?" he murmured. "I'm ready to hear anything that's new."

Lou's stubborn streak surfaced. He resented being pushed out in front like this. He was quite certain how Parnell would accept this new idea. Parnell was an opinionated and overbearing man. If an idea didn't come from him, it wasn't worth considering.

"Go ahead, Lou," Mellinger urged. "I'd like to hear what Welles has to say about this."

"We were just talking about wheat, Welles," Lou said evenly. "I was telling them that western Kansas has been doing pretty well with red Turkey wheat. It might be something to look into."

Parnell made a slash of his hand, wiping out Lou's words as thoroughly as an eraser against a blackboard.

"Just a newfangled idea," he stated positively. "Hell, even the name is foreign." His sly smile swept around the circle of listening men, inviting them to enjoy his small joke. "Things have come to a sorry pass when we start thinking about planting foreign seed."

Lou's face burned, and his temper was slipping. He had listened to other opinionated views of the banker, and they had rubbed him equally as raw. "I don't know if it's Turkey seed or not," he snapped. "Even if it is, the name doesn't mean a damned thing to me. All I'm interested in is will it produce." Lou's jaw was a hard, rigid line as he stared at Parnell.

Parnell was shaking his head, and the pitying gesture said he was listening to an addlepated man. "Damned if I'd put my money into some half-assed idea," he said loftily.

Lou was beginning to boil. It wasn't because he knew all his listeners had swung to Parnell's opinion. That didn't matter, even though it galled him. Because Parnell had money people bowed and scraped before him, and that did rasp Lou. He had to push Parnell off his pompous pedestal.

"Welles, have you seen any of this wheat?" Lou spit out the words.

Parnell was grinning because Lou was so stirred up. "No, but I don't have to see a rattlesnake to know it's bad for me."

That pulled a snicker from one of the men. Lou didn't even turn his head. He didn't care which one it was. Let all of them snicker. Before he was through, maybe that snickering would be directed at Parnell.

"You haven't seen wheat grown," he pressed on. "I doubt if you even know what it looks like. You haven't talked to anybody about growing wheat. You don't know what their costs are or their returns. You haven't the slightest idea whether wheat is a profitable or a costly thing. Yet that doesn't stop you from flapping your fat mouth. Just what in the hell makes you such a goddamned expert?"

Parnell's inhalation had a ragged sound, and his face went pinched and white. Lou had ripped him apart before all these men, and Parnell didn't have to look at any of them to know he had lost ground.

Mottled patches of red appeared in his cheeks, and he lashed out verbally at Lou. "Ah," he said mockingly, "I forgot. I'm talking to an expert in everything, the man who knows all the answers. While you're being such an expert, Lou, give us your view on women. Tell us how you keep one fooled while you're chasing another. Most of us couldn't accomplish that, but to an expert, it must be easy."

Lou choked, and a band tightened about his head. He was so furious, he couldn't see Parnell plainly. He tried to speak, and for a moment, he couldn't get a word out. So Parnell knew about his seeing Celia. Lou had been foolish to think that the entire community didn't know. Let a man wear his hat at a different angle, and the whole community spoke about it.

"Aw, Welles," Mellinger protested. "That's going pretty far."

Parnell held up a hand to check Mellinger's further words. "The way he mixes them amazes me. Everybody knows what that woman at Storhmier's is. She giving you something pretty special, Lou?"

The band was remorselessly tightening about Lou's head, and he couldn't get enough air. "Why, you rotten son of a bitch," he gasped and hit Parnell full in the face.

It was a solid blow, knocking Parnell down. He landed on his back and stared stupidly up at Lou.

The pressure around Lou's head was gone. He breathed in great gulps of air, and it ran his words together and made them jerky.

"Get up, Welles. We'll talk some more about it." He threw a withering glance around him. None of them better try to stop him or aid Parnell in any way. Parnell had earned that blow and a hell of a lot more. Lou saw no sign of interference from any of them and transferred his attention to the downed man.

He expected Parnell to get up. There wasn't that much discrepancy in their ages, and Parnell was still a solid figure of a man.

"Didn't you hear me?" Lou yelled. "I said get up." He prodded Parnell with the toe of his shoe.

Parnell's eyes were clearing. He shook his head several times, then sat up. He looked at the blood on his hand, and there was anger and humiliation in his roar.

"Why, goddamn you, if you think you can do this—"

"I just did," Lou said coldly.

Parnell tried to heave himself to his feet. His arms were too weak on the first effort, for they buckled on him, dumping him back on the ground. "You're going to pay for this," he slobbered and put his arms under him again.

Lou wanted to kick Parnell's head off, but he held himself in check.

He would let Parnell get to his feet before he tried to collect further for Parnell's remarks.

Parnell got to his feet on the third attempt. His arms dangled, and his legs kept buckling. With each sobbing breath, he sprayed flecks of blood before him. "You'll see," he said thickly.

"What's the matter, Welles?" Lou taunted him. "You don't want to talk about it any more?" Lou was ready to move in on him again.

"What the hell is going on here?" a heavy voice roared. A bulky form rushed in between Lou and Parnell. Nalley shoved at Lou and pushed him back. Nalley whirled and wrapped his arms about Parnell.

Lou clawed at Nalley, trying to pull his arms away from Parnell. "Stay out of this, Sam," he warned. "He asked for it."

"Keep that crazy man back," Nalley panted. "Goddamn it, I said break this up."

People were streaming out of the schoolhouse, drawn by the loud voices.

Lou still struggled to get at Parnell, and Nalley yelled, "Stop it, Lou. Do you want the women seeing this?"

That jarred several of the onlookers into action, and they made a solid barrier between Lou and Parnell.

"Cool down, Lou," one of them said. "It's done with."

Parnell was making halfhearted attempts to free himself from Nalley's grip.

"He hit me," Parnell babbled, "for no reason at all. By God, this isn't over yet. He'll hear from me."

"Lou, you through?" Nalley asked. His hard eyes bored into Lou.

Lou's rage was ebbing fast. The crowd was thickening around the scene, and he knew a sudden embarrassment. His desire to get at Parnell again was gone.

"He made a remark I couldn't take, Sam," he said dully.

Nalley's eyes went from face to face of the men who had witnessed the fight. "Mellinger, Tilden, Riley? Is what Lou said true?"

Mellinger scuffed the toe of his shoe in the dirt. He wouldn't look directly at Nalley. "Welles said something that was pretty raw," he muttered.

Nalley's sharp eyes went back to Lou, then he nodded.

Thank God, Lou thought. Nalley wasn't going to press this further before all these onlookers.

"Get out of here, Welles," Nalley said and released his hold on Parnell.

"I promise you this isn't done," Parnell said shrilly. "I'll prefer charges against him. He'll see—"

"Shut up," Nalley said wearily. He looked at Parnell with disgust. "Damned if you ain't a mess. I'd think you'd be glad this fight was stopped. From the looks of you, I'd say you already had more than you want."

He turned Parnell and shoved him away. Parnell stumbled two steps before he regained his balance, but he made no effort to come back at Lou. He turned a blood-smeared face over his shoulder and uttered a last futile threat. "You'll see," he said and pushed angrily through the watching crowd.

Nalley moved to Lou and said, "You were going home, weren't you, Lou?" By the tone of his voice it was an order, not a question.

"I'm going," Lou said shortly.

Nalley walked with him to where Dandy was tied. Before Lou mounted, Nalley asked, "What was that all about?"

"He butted into something that was none of his affair, Sam. We were just standing out here talking about wheat. I was telling them what I'd heard about it. Welles came up and butted in."

"You hit him for that?" Nalley asked incredulously.

Lou shook his head. He didn't want to talk about this at all, but he couldn't cut Nalley short. "He tried to make a fool out of me, and I challenged him."

"I still don't see how—"

Lou might as well tell him now; it would all come out anyway. "Sam, he tried to be smart at my expense," he said in a low voice. He couldn't look at Nalley. "He said I was an expert at handling women, that I had two on the string at once."

Those piercing eyes rested on Lou for a long moment, but Nalley made no comment. "Ah," he said and let it lay there. "Did the others hear what he said?"

Lou couldn't understand what Nalley was driving at. "They did," he admitted. "Mellinger even commented on it. I don't see what that has to do with anything."

"You may need their testimony," Nalley said softly. "Welles is a proud man. You humiliated him before quite a few people. Do you think he can forget that?"

"I don't give a good damn what he does," Lou said.

Nalley threw an arm across Lou's shoulders. "Don't bow your neck at me. I'm just suggesting what could happen. Damn it, Lou. Why did you pick the only banker in town for your ruckus?"

Lou frowned. "I don't get what you mean. What does that have to do with anything?"

Nalley gave him a lugubrious grin. "I do my banking business with him. I stepped in on your side. I made it pretty plain how I felt."

Lou was immediately conscience-stricken. "I didn't even think of that, Sam. I'm sorry—"

Nalley shrugged away Lou's concern. "I'm not saying he's going to cause me trouble, Lou. But I want you to start using your head instead of your fist."

Nalley's gravity worried Lou. "You're saying Parnell will follow through?"

"You can damn well bet on it," Nalley said firmly. "I'll bet the night isn't out before Welles goes to see Briner."

Lou's forehead was furrowed with concern. He sure didn't want the sheriff after him. He didn't know how much influence Parnell carried with Briner. But Briner was a level-headed man, and Lou had never known him to be awed by the amount of money a man had. Just the same he didn't want Briner nibbling at his ass. If Briner was determined enough, Lou was pretty certain the sheriff could find a few infractions Lou had committed that could cause trouble.

Nalley chuckled, for he sensed the worry churning around in Lou's head. "Don't fret over it too much. But you remember who those men around you were when Parnell came up. Could Parnell influence them to go against you?"

Lou was sure he knew every one of those men well. "Not a chance," he said stoutly.

"That's a relief," Nalley said. "Go on home and get some sleep. I'll see you soon."

Lou nodded, untied Dandy, and mounted. What a bust this evening had been. First, his argument with Maude and now this. Nalley must know that his daughter had been involved in Parnell's remarks, but he hadn't said a word about that. Lou groaned inwardly. He liked this man too much to want anything to come between them. He lifted his hand and waved before he turned Dandy. He wasn't going home, not right now any way. He guessed he was being a damned fool, but he wanted to see Celia again.

CHAPTER THREE

The long hitch rack before Storhmier's saloon and dance hall was filled. It always was at this hour of the night. Storhmier did a hell of a business. Lou scowled as he tied Dandy across the street. If it was the bar and gambling drawing all the owners of those horses at Storhmier's rack, Lou wouldn't mind. But he knew the attraction that drew them. Ever since Celia's arrival at Storhmier's, business had noticeably expanded. Lou couldn't blame those men. He knew how he felt toward her.

Before he entered Storhmier's door Lou was tempted to look guiltily about him. He shook the weakening impulse away. If all of the town and half of the county didn't know he was coming here as often as he could, then the remainder certainly would, after what had happened tonight. He thought of Maude, and the feeling of guilt strengthened. Lou was angry with himself. He wasn't breaking a vow of any kind, either in words or by implication. If Maude had jumped to some kind of a conclusion, Lou was sorry for her, but he wasn't going to blame himself.

Storhmier's was the most elaborate place of entertainment in the county. A man could get just about anything he wanted here. Russell, Kansas, viewed the establishment with mixed emotions. Half of the town was all for Storhmier's, arguing that a man needed such a place to relax. The other half screamed to high Heaven about its being here, saying the wicked den of evil should be stamped out. Even Reverend Simmons had preached a couple of sermons about the disgrace of such a hellhole being allowed in this town. Lou wasn't bothered much one way or the other, for he rarely went into Storhmier's until Celia came. Then his viewpoint changed drastically. Reverend Simmons and all the others who shared his view were all wrong. It was as simple as that.

Lou paused just inside the door. As usual, Storhmier's was doing a thriving business. The bar was crowded, and every gaming table was packed. Maybe Storhmier did take a considerable amount of money out of the community, but it was a man's right to spend his money the way he saw fit.

Two of the dance-hall girls looked up and saw Lou. They didn't actually shrug, but the implication was there. Lou Manard was only interested in one person here.

Lou didn't realize he was frowning. At least two dozen men were crowded around Celia's piano. Lou had never come in here when it wasn't that way. Men liked to hear her play. Besides that ability, she had a quick and ready wit to respond to any sally a man might make and turn it to his disadvantage.

Lou stood there, his eyes fastened on her. The same sensations he knew the first time he saw her were back but stronger. He had a hollow space where his stomach should be, and he was breathing harder, and his collar felt tight and too warm.

"Well, look who's here," a voice said from his left. "If it isn't the big spender himself."

Lou knew the voice before he turned to face the speaker. He should; he had heard it often enough, and his reactions were the same. He tried to keep his dislike off his face and out of his tone.

"Hello, Herrick," he said curtly.

Phil Herrick was over six feet tall, and as yet no excess fat showed on his lean frame. His face was cut with bold, decisive strokes, and Lou supposed women would find him handsome, though he didn't see any reason why. Herrick's eyes were too cold, the lips too thin. Lou couldn't see any warmth in this man at all.

Herrick had a way of looking at Lou that made Lou's skin crawl. The same look was on Herrick's face now, condescending or maybe just plain contemptuous. Lou felt the heat run up from his neck and gather in his cheeks.

"Are you going to buy another beer?" Herrick asked mockingly. "Without your business, I don't know what we would do."

"If I feel like it," Lou snapped. He wondered at the animosity that seemed to spring so quickly between them. A few months ago it hadn't been that way. Occasionally, Lou had stopped in Storhmier's, and Herrick paid him little attention. Herrick's change happened almost from the moment Celia arrived.

My God, Lou thought. Herrick's jealous over Celia. It won't do him any good, Lou assured himself. A floorman for Storhmier couldn't be making much money. What could Herrick offer somebody like Celia. Just the same a new gnawing worry went to work in Lou. He couldn't help but contrast himself physically against Herrick, and in Lou's eyes he was coming out a bad second.

Herrick dropped the mockery, and his eyes were poisonous. "You're wasting your time, farmer," he said.

Herrick's breathing was too hard, and his face was flushed. Those two things restored some of Lou's assurance.

"Maybe not," Lou said, and this time the mockery was in his voice. "I'll let her be the judge of that."

He saw the unbridled anger in Herrick's eyes before he moved away from him.

Lou found a table near Celia's piano and sat down. Celia saw him. The quick flash of welcome crossing her face told Lou that she would join him as quickly as she could.

He sat there, his eyes never leaving her. He saw only her profile, but she was something to see. Her face was carved flawlessly, and Lou listened to her playing and singing. She had a mastery of those keys, though her singing voice was on the weak side. That wasn't being critical. The thought just occurred to Lou. The quick flash of welcome in Celia's eyes told Lou he needn't worry about the competition of the men gathered around her piano, nor Herrick's either. The thought restored Lou's confidence, and he wanted to laugh aloud.

His eyes feasted on that lovely face. He didn't know whether that blondness was real or artificial, but it didn't matter. Her hair touched her cheeks with soft waves, and those blue eyes and bare shoulders were equally expressive. She was a small woman, barely topping five feet, and that was an aid to Lou's assurance. She made him feel much taller than he was.

She played for another twenty minutes before she stood and said, "That's all, right now, boys." She raised a hand at the clamor of protest. "I'll be back. That's a promise."

Lou's heart swelled with joy as she came toward his table. Every man in this big room would offer to buy her a drink, and she was accepting only Lou's offer.

He stood as she approached his table and pulled out a chair for her. He smelled her perfume as he bent over her, then straightened and walked back to his chair. He sat down before he said, "Hello, Celia."

Those expressive eyes worked on him. "I was afraid you weren't coming in tonight," she said. She had a deep, throaty voice.

"Nothing could have kept me away," he replied. Surely by now, she knew that. She looked tired tonight and it made her seem a few years older. But that didn't matter. Nothing mattered but the fact that she was here.

"You're tired," he said. "Can I order you a drink?"

She waved the offer away. "Maybe later, Lou. I am a little tired."

"Storhmier's working you too hard," Lou said in indignation.

Her shrug spoke for her. "That's what he hires me for."

She seemed disconsolate tonight, and Lou wished he could remove that feeling for her. He remembered walking into Storhmier's that first night, and there was Storhmier's new singer and piano player. Looking at Celia was like being struck with lightning. Lou couldn't take his eyes off her. Love couldn't happen this fast, he argued with himself, but here it was. That feeling had only grown on successive visits.

Enthralled, Lou had spent hours listening to her talk. She spoke knowingly of so many places. She had traveled so widely. The towns and cities she named were just that; names. Lou would never see a fraction of those places.

He remembered how her eyes sparkled once when she spoke of San Francisco, and he mentioned the city again tonight, wanting to see the life return to those eyes.

Celia reached over and covered Lou's hand with hers. "It's not as wonderful as I make it sound. I know all those places, but not a single part of them is mine. I can call off their streets, but that doesn't change the fact that I'm a stranger. I know them for a few weeks, then I'm off again. I never have enough time to get to know them really well. God," she finished passionately, "I'm growing to hate traveling." She made a face at him. "I won't feel as much loss when I leave Russell." She laughed ruefully. "It's not really big enough to even remember."

The thought of her leaving stabbed fear through Lou. He hadn't given it much thought, but in her itinerant business, she would never light long in one place.

"Storhmier won't let you go," he said positively. "You're too good for business."

She wrinkled her nose at him, and some of her depressed mood seemed to lighten. "But who knows when that will be? People look for a change in everything."

"Not me," he said firmly. "I'd be content to look at you forever."

Her cheeks colored with pleasure, and she looked squarely at him. "In a way, I envy you, Lou. You've put down roots. You know what you'll be doing this year and the next. You know where you belong. That's more than I can say."

Her words emboldened Lou, and he found an eloquence he usually didn't have. "You don't have to leave, Celia. You could just stay here. All the traveling would be over." He couldn't stop his words from picking up speed. He was afraid she would laugh in his face.

Celia leaned across the table and brushed the back of her fingers across his cheek. "You don't know how enticing that sounds, Lou."

Her words were all the encouragement Lou needed. Now, he could say what was in his mind. "I mean it, Celia." He had never talked better, painting a glowing picture of living on a farm. "You'd find where you belong. You wouldn't be working for anybody else, Celia. Next year and all the years after, you'd know where you belong."

Her breathing quickened, and a mist seemed to dim the ordinary brightness in her eyes. She tried to say it archly, but the tremor in her voice gave her away. "Why, Lou, that sounds like a proposal to me."

"It is," he said stoutly. "I've never had better prospects than this year. My corn looks better at this stage than I've ever seen it. This is going to be a big year. And the following ones will be bigger. I feel it in my bones." Lou would never have believed he could get those words out. He watched her anxiously, waiting for a reaction.

She shook her head, but there was no real denial in the gesture. "How attractive you make it all sound."

"All you have to do is to say yes," he said.

Her laugh was shaky, and the mist didn't leave her eyes. "You're sweet, Lou, but you don't give a girl a chance to catch her breath."

Her wavering encouraged Lou. "All you have to do is to say yes," he pointed out.

"Lou, you've got to give me time to think," she protested.

Lou's laughter was buoyant and happy. She was leaning his way, he could tell. "Take all the time you want. I'll be back tomorrow night for your answer."

She looked a little dazed at the whirlwind turn of events. "I'm not promising you a thing," she said faintly.

"Just think that you're home," Lou said. "You'll never have to travel again."

He was wise enough not to press her further at the moment. Let everything he had said run around in her mind. They would do all the pressing that was necessary.

"Here comes Storhmier," she said suddenly. "I guess he thinks it's time for me to get back to work."

Lou squeezed her hand before he stood. "Tomorrow night," he repeated.

He passed Herrick on the way out. He had never seen so much poison in a man's eyes. Lou wanted to chuckle. He marched past Herrick, feeling taller than he had ever felt in his life.

Herrick came over to Celia the next time she had a few free moments. "I want to talk to you," he growled. He stalked to a table and sat down, glowering into space. He didn't say another word until Celia sat across from him.

"That was a touching little scene between you and the hick," he said caustically.

Celia's eyes brightened. "Ah, so you noticed," she murmured. She had thought of nothing but Lou's words the past two hours. She had no intention of considering them seriously, but still it was pleasant to think she could get out of this life, if she wanted to. So Herrick was jealous. She was aware of how much his eyes rested on her, but until now she wasn't sure how he felt. Herrick's jealousy now showed, and that could be used to her advantage.

"You're jealous, Phil," Celia said and laughed.

Herrick looked affronted. "Me jealous of that farmer," he scoffed.

"Maybe you should be, Phil. Lou just proposed to me."

Herrick slammed his fist on the table. He should have known something like that was happening by the new shine in her eyes.

"My God, no," Herrick said in violent protest. He snorted his disbelief. "I can't believe it. You cut him off short, didn't you?"

She shook her head, a mocking smile on her lips.

A new fear gripped Herrick. He had known a lot of women in his life, but this one had hit him hard. He thought he had been making time with her until Manard came in here.

"You're kidding," Herrick said hoarsely.

Her face stiffened. "Why do you find it so impossible, Phil?"

The fear took a harder grip on Herrick, making his words jerky. "Good Lord, Celia. It isn't possible that you can be taking him seriously. Why, you live in another world. Can you see yourself as a farmer's wife?" He tried to laugh, and it came out squeaky, showing the depth of the fear in him.

"Maybe I can, Phil. Do you find that amusing?" she asked quietly.

Herrick leaned back in his chair, getting control of his emotions. He had let her see how vulnerable he was, and that weakened his position.

"Very amusing," he said dryly. "I can just see you wearing feed-grain-sack dresses as you feed the chickens." He laughed again, this time with more assurance. His eyes swept over her. "Oh, that'd be a sight."

That stung her, for color filled her face. "Maybe you're right for now," she conceded in a frozen voice. "But it won't always be that way. He told me of his prospects." The mocking grin remained on Herrick's lips, and she had to wipe it away. "Lou told me his corn crop never looked better." She searched her mind, trying to remember some of the things Lou had told her. She had to shake Herrick. "He's fattening some steers for the fall market. He isn't poor." Her tone picked up a new bite. "Do you think I would be any worse off than I am now?"

"You answer that for yourself, Celia," Herrick said as he rose from the table. The rage was making him shake inwardly. He leaned toward her and stabbed a finger in her face. "Why hell, you wouldn't last a week living like that. You'd come flying back, begging Storhmier to take you back."

Celia's face was smug with assurance. She had him now. She didn't need Herrick pointing out how unsuitable a farm wife's life was for her, but it was reassuring to know that two men were interested in her. It opened up a new horizon, relieving the pressure she sometimes felt.

"We'll see, Phil," she said, smiling at him.

Herrick's face was black as he strode away from the table.

CHAPTER FOUR

Herrick spent a miserable night, tossing and turning. In the morning, he cut himself twice while shaving, and he never did that. My God, his shakiness was showing. Could Celia be serious about what she said last night? Each time he asked himself that question, he answered with a violent "No." But just the same, the worry remained. Had that damned farmer been able to put glamour in the life he proposed? The memory of Celia's smile had to make Herrick consider that.

The blood welled up again from the last cut, and Herrick wiped it away. Until this moment, he hadn't known just how badly he wanted Celia. He couldn't just let things lie the way they were. He had to do something about breaking up Celia's relationship with Manard.

His frown deepened as he dressed. He couldn't offer Celia much. Storhmier wasn't an overly generous man when it came to paying salaries. Herrick could barely stretch out his earnings from one week to the next. His face burned as he thought of how he would stand against what Manard offered.

He tugged on his boots, his thoughts darting about like trapped mice. Maybe that damned Manard lied to her, maybe he had overblown his prospects. Herrick had seen too many Kansas farms. Their owners earned barely enough to carry them from one year to the next. But some of those farmers weren't doing too badly, a stubborn little thought persisted. Well, there was one way to disprove that stubborn thought; go out and see how Manard was doing.

Herrick adjusted the tilt of his hat before the mirror, stared long and soberly at his reflection before he turned for the door. Physically, it wasn't hard to see how he stood against Manard. Herrick could say without bragging that it was like comparing a fine-blooded horse against a mule. He grinned bleakly at the comparison. Celia wasn't a moonstruck girl. She had knocked around on her own for quite a few years now. She had acquired enough cynical wisdom to know that looks alone put little food on the table.

Herrick's jaw was a rigid line as he walked out of the room. Maybe riding out and seeing what Manard had wouldn't do him any real good, but at least, he would have a better estimate of his competition.

He nodded to Mrs. Schindler as he left the boardinghouse. She was a gaunt woman with a suspicious glint in her eyes. The years of trying to wrest a profit out of this boardinghouse had etched cruel lines in her face. Herrick had learned quite a while back that she wouldn't wait even a day for her rent. If he was even a day late, he knew she would pitch him out. Almost half of what he made went for his board and lodging. It was a damned, rough world, and nobody gave away anything for nothing. Celia should know that.

" 'Morning, Mrs. Schindler," he said.

He grinned cynically as he walked out of the house. She must be in a good mood today, for she answered his greeting with a sniff.

Herrick walked the two blocks to Stricker's stable. Stricker was busy cleaning a stall when Herrick walked in. He was a broad-shouldered man with big, gnarled hands, and he attacked his work vigorously. Why shouldn't he, Herrick thought disconsolately. He's working for himself.

He watched Stricker work for a few moments before he interrupted him. How did a man accumulate enough money to go into business for himself? Herrick was nearing thirty, and he hadn't been able to save enough money to even think of going into business. He sure as hell wouldn't pick something like this. It was too much work.

Stricker straightened to catch a breath, and Herrick said, "Hello, Cal."

Stricker turned, his heavy face creasing in a smile. "Hello, Phil," he returned. "I didn't expect to see you here."

Herrick flushed at the implication in Stricker's voice. He didn't even own a horse. There was little likelihood Herrick would ever be a customer of Stricker's.

"Cal, I'm looking for directions to get out to the Manard place."

"Which one?" Stricker asked. "There's two of them, father and son."

Herrick knew it was the son he wanted to hear about, but he was curious about any information he could gather about the Manards. "Both of them farmers?" he asked.

Stricker chuckled. "Don't let Doyle Manard hear you ask that. He's about the only real cattleman we've got left around here."

"Ah," Herrick said to hide the disappointment he felt. Just the term "cattleman" denoted money. It sounded as though Lou had solid backing behind him.

"How come Lou is a farmer?" Herrick asked.

A shadow clouded Stricker's eyes. Evidently, he didn't put out information readily about the neighbors.

"You can ask Lou that," he said flatly.

Herrick took the rebuke without resentment. "How do I get out to Lou's place?" Herrick asked. "Or can't you tell me that?"

Stricker's face didn't change under the sarcasm. "Take the road due east out of town. About eight miles. Big, old house with two huge maple trees in the yard. Those trees are the talk of the county. Damned valuable things with trees so scarce in these parts. You figure on walking out there?" he asked sardonically.

Herrick's jaw tightened. Stricker was paying him back for his sarcasm. "I want to rent a horse," he said curtly.

"Sure," Stricker replied, but he hesitated.

Herrick knew what he was waiting for, and his eyes smoldered. Stricker was waiting for payment before he went after the horse.

Herrick pulled a few bills out of his pocket. "Are you afraid I didn't have it?" he snapped.

"Just making sure," Stricker said cheerfully. "How long do you figure you'll be gone?"

"Two or three hours." The curtness remained in Herrick's voice.

Stricker took two dollars out of Herrick's hand. "This will cover it."

He was gone for only a few minutes, then came back, leading an old, dispirited horse.

"Why, damn it," Herrick flared. "I'm not renting a plug like that."

Stricker's eyes weighed Herrick. Some of the cheerfulness was gone from his expression. "The only thing I have left is only half broken. I didn't figure you could—" He gestured vaguely and left the sentence unfinished.

Herrick knew what Stricker had in mind. Stricker thought of him as a town man, incapable of handling a spirited animal.

"Bring it out," Herrick said savagely.

Stricker nodded, his jaw grim. "You asked for it."

He came back, leading a moon-eyed piebald. The piebald pulled back on the reins, snorting nervously.

"He can be rough," Stricker warned, as Herrick put his foot in the stirrup.

"I'll worry about that," Herrick said and swung up. He was glad the runway was unusually wide. He had seen moon-eyed horses go completely wild, crashing blindly into anything in their paths.

The piebald hunched under Herrick, and Herrick was sorry he wasn't wearing spurs. It was almost a certainty he would need them before he mannered this brute.

The piebald came out of a crouching hump in a jump that seemed as though it was going to carry Herrick through the roof. The horse came down, landing in the prints he had left. It squalled in fury, and Herrick's eyes gleamed. That mannering was going to take some doing. He drove his heels savagely into the horse's flanks. Now, he regretted his lack of spurs more than ever. A little raking of the steel changed an ornery horse's mind in a hurry.

The piebald was a rough bucker, but he didn't need a lot of room to put up a fight. Herrick had known buckers before that needed half a county, but this one came down in the space of a few yards. The piebald put fury into its bucks, but lacked stamina. The horse tired after a half-dozen bucks and stood on widely spraddled legs, its head drooping.

Stricker looked up at Herrick with undisguised admiration. "That's not your first bucker."

Herrick enjoyed that admiration. It had been so long since he had known that feeling. "Hell, Cal, I used to ride rougher ones than this for a living. What's his name?"

"Caesar," Stricker replied.

Herrick's grin broadened. "Well, Caesar didn't last long, either."

He touched his boot heels against the horse's flanks, and Caesar moved out willingly enough. Herrick didn't mind orneriness in a horse as long as it didn't go into bone-deep cussedness. When you found that in a horse, you had to keep your eyes open, for those kind of outlaws were always seeking some way to pay you back.

What Herrick said to Stricker about riding this kind of horse for a living was true. For five years, the rough ones of the remuda had been turned over to him, and he'd done one hell of a job turning them back to the ranch ready to ride.

For several minutes, his eyes were unseeing as he relived those days. Did he regret they were over? He shrugged in sudden irritation. It was a different time, a different place, and all the youth was gone now. He had been badly busted up in his last attempt with a bucker, and it had taken him almost a year to recover. The ownership of the ranch had dropped out from under him long before that year was over. It had been rough, getting along without a regular salary. The busted-up leg had mended, but he dragged it for quite a while. Even now in bad weather, there was an ache in the leg, recalling the old days.

Herrick remembered that time too well. He had drifted from town to town, scrounging any job he could to keep alive. A year and a half ago, Storhmier had hired him as a floorman. At the time, Herrick was damned glad to get the job, but since he had seen Celia, the job was no longer adequate.

He squirmed as he felt the pressure again squeezing his guts. If there was a better way of making a living, he hadn't found it. He learned early that gambling wasn't the answer for him. He was too cautious, squeezing his money too tightly, and Lady Luck never looked favorably on that kind of player.

Herrick leaned over and patted Caesar's neck, knowing almost an affection for the animal. It brought back the old days when he was somebody important and men looked up to him. He had seen just a flash of that in Stricker's eyes. It was good to have it back again, if only for a moment.

"We'll go out and see what this damned farmer has," Herrick said. Maybe his earlier training had implanted a deep dislike for the plowmen. Herrick grinned twistedly. Celia's interest in Lou Manard hadn't done anything to lessen that dislike.

He noticed everything he passed with an observing eye. The crops looked good, too good. Maybe Manard wasn't boasting when he spoke of his prospects.

Herrick decided that was Manard's house ahead. Stricker had said the two maple trees would make it stand out. It was a solidly built house, constructed by a man who had permanence in mind. The house was weatherbeaten until it blended well with its surroundings. Manard couldn't have built it. The house was far older than that.

Herrick looked it over with loathing. It was a far better house than many of the farmhouses he had seen in this country. Damn it, that was all to the bad. He hoped to be able to go back and tell Celia what a shack Lou lived in. The barn behind the house was well built, too.

Herrick didn't dawdle as he passed the house. He didn't want Lou coming out and seeing him. His face was set in a heavy scowl as he went on down the road. So far this trip was a complete bust. He hadn't seen anything that would let him tell Celia that Lou Manard was a liar.

The cornfield started a few hundred yards beyond the house, and that was a knife twisting in Herrick's heart. He was no farmer, but even to his unpracticed eye, this corn looked good.

He beat his clenched fist into his leg. Oh, goddamn it. Everything was working against him.

The road ended abruptly against a gate. Herrick looked out at the land beyond. Now, this was familiar, this was grazing land. To bolster his impression, he saw a half-dozen cows grazing just beyond the fence.

That had to be Doyle Manard's land. He wondered dispiritedly why Lou had ever split away from his father. Herrick snorted in disgust. He couldn't imagine anybody choosing farming over cattle raising.

Herrick swung down, and holding Caesar's reins, led him to the gate. He opened it and led Caesar through. This was trespassing but if he was caught on this land, he could simply say he lost his way.

He remounted and rode along the far end of the cornfield, his unhappiness growing. Damned big field. No wonder Lou could speak so glowingly to Celia of his prospects.

A hell of a poor fence, he thought, as he rode along beside it. Those fence posts looked rotten, and Herrick didn't see what kept those cows out of this corn. He knew how much cows liked fresh, young corn.

Herrick's eyes widened as the thought struck him. Wouldn't it be a shame, if those cows broke through into Manard's cornfield? Why, they could do a hell of a lot of damage in a short time, maybe enough to wipe out Manard's prospects of a good crop.

Herrick breathed hard as he stepped off and tethered Caesar to a fence post. He moved on foot to the next post and leaned tentatively against it. It didn't take much pressure to break it off at the ground. Herrick grinned fiendishly as he thought, if twenty or so of these posts snapped off this easily, it would leave a wide open path for those cows.

He walked from post to post, snapping them off, leaving a tangled mass of broken posts and twisted wires behind him. Cows wouldn't have any trouble at all crossing that space, particularly if they were encouraged a little.

Herrick's breathing was faster, as he hurried back to Caesar and remounted. He saw more cows, maybe as many as thirty or forty. Now, it was time to give those cows the help they needed in finding that break.

He rounded them up, moving them slowly, chousing them easily toward the fence. A cow was a stubborn brute, particularly if it was pressed, but if a man took it easy, he could generally drive them in the direction he wanted.

Herrick kept glancing nervously about him as he worked. If he was found doing this, there would be no explanation at all. He was sweating hard by the time the first few cows went through the break.

He pulled Caesar to a stop, threw back his head, and laughed in wicked satisfaction. Get the leaders through the break, and nothing could stop the others. Herrick wished he could see Manard's face when he discovered those cows in his cornfield. That was a luxury he couldn't afford. Right now, he'd better get the hell out of here.

CHAPTER FIVE

Lou lifted his head as he heard the hoof beats. This was the second rider he had heard this morning, and that was a lot of traffic down this road in a morning. He had been greasing the cultivator. He wasn't pressed for time, but another cultivation of the corn was coming up.

Lou wiped the grease from his hands with a gunny bag, as he walked out of the barn to see who this rider was. He hadn't caught more than a glimpse of the first man who passed his place earlier. The eastern sun was in his eyes, and Lou hadn't gotten much more than a hazy impression of a tall man. He had the odd feeling that it was Phil Herrick. He had shaken his head in disbelief. Why would Herrick be out this way? But this rider had stopped, and Lou better check to see who it was.

He came around the house, and his face fell as he saw Sam Nalley dismount before the porch. Sure, he was always glad to see Nalley but not under these circumstances. A certain uneasy feeling told him last night's argument with Maude was the reason for this visit.

"Hello, Sam." He tried to put brightness into the greeting, but it had a false ring.

" 'Morning, Lou," Nalley returned.

Lou caught his breath. Ah, something was wrong. Nalley avoided looking directly at Lou.

"Something wrong, Sam?" he asked quietly.

"Why should there be?" Nalley's quick glance was harried. "Just found myself all caught up and thought I'd ride over for a little visit."

Lou knew that wasn't the reason behind Nalley's visit, for Nalley had never been good at being evasive.

"Spit it out, Sam," Lou said levelly. He wanted this out in the open, but Nalley had to open up the talk.

Nalley dug a hole in the ground with the toe of his shoe. He was having too much trouble getting his words out.

Lou waited patiently. He wasn't going to give Nalley any help.

"You and Maude have an argument last night?" Nalley blurted out. This time he looked squarely at Lou.

"Did she say so?" Lou asked carefully.

"Not in so many words." Nalley's eyes begged Lou for understanding. "But I knew something was wrong by the way she acted. Not a word all the way home last night and nothing this morning. I tried to get her to talk, but she just clamped her mouth. Lou, is there some trouble between you two? If there is, I want to do everything I can to straighten it out."

"There was no trouble," Lou said flatly. God, how he dreaded saying what was in his mind, but he'd never been a devious man, and he wasn't going to start now with Nalley.

"Sam, there was no trouble. Not in the way you mean. Maude and you and Sarah did nothing to offend me." It was hard to keep looking directly at Nalley. "Sam, I never promised Maude a thing. I know I was seeing her, but—" His words faltered, and he made a vague gesture. This was harder to say than he thought.

"But you just found somebody else," Nalley said in a low voice.

Lou dared look at him. Nalley was grinning, but painfully.

"I guess that's about it, Sam."

For a moment, Nalley's face tightened. He was showing a lot of stress. "Celia?" he asked.

Nalley raised a hand against the indignation forming in Lou's face. "Talk gets around, Lou. I've heard her name mentioned with yours. You've been seeing her a lot lately." The words were dull, but there was no accusation in them.

Lou let out a ragged breath. He wanted to tell Nalley he proposed to Celia last night, but the words stuck in his throat.

"Hell, Lou, I understand," Nalley said heavily. "She's a good-looking woman. It just happens that way sometimes to a man." His grin returned, and it was truer this time. "Damn it, Lou, a man can't help the way something hits him."

"I didn't want anything to stand between us, Sam."

"You can forget about that," Nalley said stoutly. "It won't, unless we let it." He peered at Lou. "Ain't that about right?"

Lou nodded. He prayed Nalley was right, but that depended upon how events turned out. The Lord knew, he didn't want animosity between him and the Nalleys.

"Lou, you know it's been over a month since I've seen those steers of yours. I'd like to see how they're doing."

Nalley was doing his best to smooth over an awkward moment, and Lou said gruffly, "Let's go look at them." He was getting over this rough spot far more easily than he had hoped.

It was a short walk to the pasture where the steers were, and Lou and Nalley spoke of crops and cattle, carefully avoiding any personal topics. Lou thought sorrowfully, it has to be this way. Their relationship was bound to be strained, at least, for a while. All Lou could do was to wait and see if the rough spots smoothed out or grew worse.

Lou leaned on the gate going into the pasture, and waved his hand at the twenty-five head of steers, grazing nearby. "What do you think of them, Sam?" He made no attempt to keep the pride out of his voice. He had every right to be proud of them.

Nalley looked at the steers speculatively. "As good a looking bunch as I ever looked at, Lou. You picked well. They look like they were all dropped by the same cow. I swear I can see the weight they've put on since the last time I saw them."

Lou grinned at the praise. "I figure they'll be ready to go before the year's out. I won't try to feed them through the winter. I hope they'll make me a few dollars."

Nalley spat on the ground. "How can they miss? I think you were smart to branch out from just raising crops." He shook his head sadly. "Wish I had money to do the same. And the foresight," he finished.

His eyes were weighing as he looked at Lou. "You're turning out to be one hell of a farmer. I wouldn't be surprised before you're through, you'll wind up showing us old-timers how it should be done." His voice roughened. "I can't see where you've made very many false steps so far."

Lou ducked his head. Nalley was really heaping praise on him. "Aw, Sam, just a lot of luck."

"Some," Nalley admitted. "In this business, a man has to have his share of that. But more than luck's behind you." The speculation in his eyes was stronger than ever. "I've never been able to figure how some men are particularly blessed, while the others struggle to find their next meal."

"Aw, Sam, cut it out," Lou said awkwardly.

Nalley chuckled. "If that makes you uncomfortable, it's because it's too damned near the truth. I want to see your corn."

There was silence between them as they walked toward Lou's cornfield. Lou had a right to be proud of this corn, but remembering Nalley's former words, he felt uncomfortable. Nalley wasn't buttering him up for some individual reason; Nalley was too honest a man for that.

"I'll be goddamned," Nalley said softly, as he looked out over the cornfield. "I swear your corn's a foot higher than mine."

"Can't be," Lou said reasonably. "We planted at the same time and used the same kind of seed."

His eyes swept over the field. He wouldn't be bragging when he said he was proud of this field. "About ready for another cultivation, Sam." He started to say something else and choked.

"Jesus Christ," he yelled. "I've got cows in this field."

Nalley followed Lou's pointing finger. It was easy to pick out the red and white splotches of color at the far end of the field. From here, he couldn't get an accurate count of the invaders, but there were more than enough to make a man sick to his stomach.

"My God," Nalley said appalled. "Where did they come from?" He was sure he knew, but he wanted Lou to say it.

"Pa's cows," Lou said bitterly. "I knew that fence between us was bad, but I thought it'd take me through the growing season." This was treeless country, and fence posts were hard to come by. Something like this always happened when a man put off a chore he knew needed doing.

"Take it easy, Lou," Nalley advised. "If we go at them too hard, we'll scatter them all over the field."

Lou wanted to yell at him but held his temper. Didn't Nalley think he knew that?

Lou and Nalley moved slowly through the field, spreading a good distance apart. The trouble was that Lou didn't know where the break was, but if they could get these cattle turned and headed in the right direction before they could bolt, the cows might find the break they came through and go back out.

Lou was so furious that he was shaking inwardly. A cow brute could do enough damage by eating the young corn. They wrapped their tongues around the stalk near the ground, gave a slight tug, and the young plant, roots and all was yanked out of the ground. But they could do even more damage with those trampling hoofs, breaking over the stalks. He wanted to run at those cows and swear at the top of his voice. God, if he had a scatter gun, he'd pepper some of those worthless hides.

Lou and Nalley advanced slowly, taking just a few cautious steps at a time. Nalley talked to the cows in a soothing voice, "Ho, boss.

Move." Every now and then, he flung out an arm to cut off a threatened move that would carry an animal deeper into the field.

Lou was so mad he couldn't speak. It was a good thing he had Nalley with him. It kept him from rushing at the cows, raving at the top of his voice. He hadn't as yet gotten an accurate count, but he was sure there were more than thirty cows in his field.

Several of the cows were now aware of Lou and Nalley's advance, for they raised their heads, looking curiously at them. So far, Lou saw no incipient break in them. Some of those cows had pieces of green corn stalk hanging from their mouths. Just seeing that was more than enough to make a man explode. Cows had a taste for young, green corn. The appetite was worse than a drunk's craving for whiskey.

Lou could see the trampling damage now. Every time a cow planted a hoof on a new stalk, it broke under the massive weight. It took hard discipline for Lou to control his impulse to rush the cows, trying to get them out as fast as he could. But that would be the worst thing he could do. A rush would put fear in the cows, and they would break into full flight. Two men weren't much of a wall against these many animals. If the animals were aroused to panic, they would easily break by Lou and Nalley and go charging through the rest of the field. Plus the additional damage they would cause, it would be pure hell trying to round them up and get them headed in the right direction.

Lou forced himself to talk to them in a soft voice as he moved forward. That old bitch was beginning to throw her head. Lou swore if she broke by him, he would run her down and break her neck.

That slow, steady advance made up the cow's mind, for she suddenly whirled and raced toward the fence. At least, that was in the general direction of the break. Lou knew he would find a big portion of the fence down. There had to be with this many cows in his field.

He looked over at Nalley and managed a sour grin. They were winning, for the other cows were turning in the right direction and following the lead cow. Nalley must have known what that grin cost Lou, for he shook his head in sympathy. Sure, Lou thought grumpily. He can stay calm. He's not looking at his corn trampled into the ground.

Lou saw the long portion of the fence down just ahead. The lead cow ran through the break, kicked up her heels, then raced onto her own range.

That was enough to make up the other brutes' minds. They whirled and followed their leader, buck jumping with every step.

Lou ran the last few steps after the cows just as they reached the break. It was safe enough now to vent his real feelings. He flailed his arms and cursed the cows in a voice loud enough to be heard in the next county.

"Get out of here, you stupid sons-a-bitches," Lou yelled after them. His face looked as though he'd been out far too long under a hot sun. He used every cuss word in his vocabulary and didn't stop until he was breathless.

Nalley shook his head in admiration. "You never missed a word," he commented.

Lou came close to yelling at him. Nalley would be swearing too, if this was his corn.

"Look at it," Lou said bitterly. Maybe the damaged area wasn't large, but every abused stalk hurt Lou. None of them would bear this season. He couldn't help but think of all the work that had gone into the planting and the hopes that had been dashed.

"You're lucky we came out here when we did," Nalley said practically. "My God, Lou, think of what those cows could have done, if they'd been allowed to stay in here a day or two."

Lou shuddered at the suggestion. If that had happened, he could count the bushels of corn he would harvest on the fingers of his hands.

Nalley gingerly raised one of the snapped off posts. The barbed wires were still attached to it. A man used every precaution handling barbed wire, for every careless movement cost him a nick or a slash.

"Broken off at the ground," he observed. "Looks like some cow leaned her weight against the post, and it couldn't hold."

Lou nodded grudgingly. That would be his guess. Cows loved to use fence posts to ease the itching in their hides. He stared down the line of posts on the ground. My God, there were so many of them. It looked as though those damned cows, acting on a simultaneous signal, had chosen an individual post and worked on it. Lou couldn't accept that. There wasn't that much intelligence in a cow brute's head.

He walked along the downed section. Twenty posts had been snapped off, and all in a line. It wasn't plausible that animals had enough sense to pick just this section without skipping a few posts. Lou could believe that the cows could have worked on a post here and there. But if so, they would have surged in over that small break without waiting to demolish a farther stretch of the fence.

Nalley had followed him, and he looked curiously at Lou. Something was working in Lou's head.

Lou bent over and lifted one of the posts for closer examination.

This one was pretty stout. The rottenness hadn't gone through the post, for it was splintered, showing some strength remained in it.

A thought was forming in Lou's mind, and he shook his head against its ridiculousness. He was beginning to think that human hands had worked on this fence, leaning weight on the posts until they snapped off or splintered.

"Something's eating on you," Nalley commented.

"Sam, I don't think the cows broke all these posts."

Nalley was startled, but he still didn't understand what Lou was driving at. "You're going to have to say it plainer for me."

Lou drew a deep breath. He knew how foolish he was going to sound, but the notion was lodged more firmly in his mind than ever.

"Sam, earlier this morning, a rider passed my place. I was working in the barn. I didn't get out in time to see for sure who it was. But it looked like Phil Herrick to me. I got busy and didn't hear him come back."

Nalley still looked at Lou, and Lou said impatiently, "Phil Herrick. He works at Storhmier's."

"I know who he is, Lou. But this still doesn't make any sense to me. Are you saying you think Herrick broke off these posts? Good God," he exploded. "What good would that do him? You're grabbing at straws, Lou."

"Maybe," Lou said curtly. The stubbornness had hardened his jaw. He thought he knew what good this would do Herrick, but he didn't put it into words. That would make Nalley hoot at him more than ever. Just the same, he was going to ask Herrick some pointed questions about this the next time he saw him.

Nalley looked at the blaze in Lou's eyes and didn't press the matter further. He knew Lou too well. Once Lou got an idea lodged in his mind, nothing knocked it out.

"We've got to do something about this fence, Lou," he said.

For a moment helplessness swept over Lou as he looked at the downed fence. He didn't have a decent replaceable post on his place, and there was no source from which to cut them.

Nalley guessed at what was in Lou's mind, for he said, "I haven't got any posts, either. But this has got to be fixed. Once we leave it, those cows will be back. Let them get a taste of green corn—" He finished his sentence by lifting his hands and letting them fall.

"I know all that," Lou said with grim impatience. "I'm going to have to go to the limestone rock country and quarry out some new posts."

The thought of the work involved didn't pull that groan out of Nalley; it was the thought of how much time that would take.

"How are we going to protect this field until a new fence is put in?"

Lou was grateful to Nalley for that "we." He could always depend upon Nalley.

"Sam, will you stay here and turn those cows, if they attempt to enter again? I'm going to talk to Pa about this."

Nalley knew Doyle Manard pretty well, too. "You think he'll listen to you?"

"He'll listen," Lou said grimly.

Lou started out, and Nalley cried, "Are you going to walk? Your father's house is over a mile from here."

Lou paused for a moment. "It would take as much time to go back to the barn and get saddled up. I can walk it. Be back as soon as I can, Sam." He resumed his long stride, never looking back at Nalley. A lot of puzzled thoughts must be running through Nalley's mind now.

CHAPTER SIX

Lou passed the marauding bunch of cows. They hadn't gone too far, and Lou knew he wouldn't be out of sight before they started wandering back toward the corn. Nalley could keep them out, but it would be only a temporary solution. Part of this was Doyle's problem. He had to move those cows so far they couldn't come up against that weakened fence again, or throw up a temporary fence. Lou didn't care which. He knew Doyle wouldn't like it, but Lou expected that. Crossing Doyle Manard in any manner never set very well with him.

The farther Lou walked the angrier he grew. He was as positive as he could be without facts to back it up that Herrick had meddled with that fence. Lou couldn't blame Nalley for thinking this was pretty far-fetched, but that was because Lou couldn't give him the reason behind his thinking. Whoa, an inner voice cautioned. Maybe you're laying blame on Herrick when it doesn't belong there. How would Herrick know about the corn?

Lou stopped, his eyes widening. Celia knew, for Lou had bragged a little about his prospects. She could easily have told Herrick what Lou said. Lou's eyes darkened. "Wait a minute," the inner voice cautioned again. She could be completely innocent of any wrongdoing. In her enthusiasm at Lou's words, she had repeated them to Herrick. Herrick saw an opportunity to hurt Lou.

Lou breathed easier at the plausible solution. It still didn't mean that he wasn't going to say a few hot words to Herrick about this. Maybe Herrick would deny it, but there were other little indications that betrayed a man.

Lou picked up his pace again. He was sweating hard by the time he reached Doyle's house. He walked up to the door and called, "Anybody home?"

"Back here," Doyle answered.

The voice came from the corral behind the house. "Damn it," Doyle said wrathfully. "Hold him still."

Lou heard the outraged squeal of a horse as he walked toward the corral, followed by the hard slamming of hoofs against the ground. Whatever was happening to that horse he didn't like.

Simmer down, Lou warned himself. Doyle was already in an angry mood. Slamming into him head-on wasn't going to help matters. Lou needed his help too badly to further enrage him.

Lou climbed up on the corral poles. Two of Doyle's riders were with Doyle. They had ropes on a horse, and both were sweating and straining. Doyle's face was an angry red. He danced around the laboring men, a small jar in his hand.

"Hold him still," he yelled again. "Every time I get ready to smear this salve on that cut, you let up on him."

Lou winced as he climbed down into the corral. All this had a familiar ring. Doyle was always short-tempered when something thwarted his wishes.

Lou walked up to Doyle and asked casually, "Need any help?"

Doyle's hot eyes swept over Lou. "Damned fool horse got into barbed wire. I'm trying to doctor the cut, but he won't stand still."

"So I gathered," Lou said dryly. The thought of losing more time drove him wild, but helping Doyle out could be the quickest way to get his attention. "Looks like you're going to have to dump him."

"There's another rope on that post over there," Doyle said caustically. "Maybe we need a farmer to show us our business."

"Could be," Lou said without rancor. He got the rope and spun out a loop. It had been quite a time since he used a rope, but as a kid he was pretty fair. Lou could just imagine Doyle's scathing comments, if he was a complete bust.

Lou waited until the horse rose on its hind legs and lashed out with its forehoofs. He judged his throw and made his cast. The loop sailed true, settling down around the forehoofs. Lou quickly tightened it. He jerked the front legs from under the horse as it came down, and the animal fell hard.

Lou gave him no slack as he ran down the rope. He sat on the horse's head and twisted an ear. He looked up at Doyle and said sardonically, "He's still. You can go ahead now."

Doyle dipped out some of the salve. "God, how I hate barbed wire," he grumbled. "I can remember a time when a man didn't have to put up with it."

But that was a long time ago, Lou thought. He had certainly picked a bad time to bring up the subject of Doyle's cows breaking into his corn.

The wire cut was a bad one on the horse's off foreshoulder, but Lou thought it looked worse than it actually was. As far as he could see, no muscles or ligaments had been damaged. A horse went crazy when he got into barbed wire. He fought it until he literally cut himself to pieces. Doyle was lucky this cut was no worse.

Doyle liberally smeared the salve on the cut, then grunted, "I guess that does it."

Lou loosened his loop and threw it off before he let go of the ear. He jumped nimbly to his feet and scurried out of the way. This horse might come up fighting mad.

The two cowhands flipped off their restraining loops, and the horse raced to the far side of the corral. He remained there, his eyes rolling. He had all he wanted from men for the time being.

"You did pretty good," Doyle said grudgingly to Lou. His eyes turned suspicious. "This a social visit, or you got something else on your mind?"

"Something else," Lou returned gravely. "Your cows tore down some of my fence and got into my corn." Maybe it wasn't actually true that Doyle's cows had gotten into the field without human help, but Lou knew his father too well. If he told Doyle his suspicions, Doyle would roar, "Then why come to me? Go get him." Lou needed Doyle's help.

Color flooded Doyle's face. "That weak stretch of fence between us?"

Lou nodded. "The same one, Pa. Nalley and I drove out thirty-five cows. He's there now, keeping guard to be sure they don't come back."

That purplish hue was growing deeper in Doyle's face. "I guess you came here to claim damages from me?"

Lou shook his head. "Not that at all, Pa. I need your help. Nalley and I can't stand guard all night. Until that fence is repaired that field is open. I'm not stewing about the damage, Pa. They ate some and trampled down some more. But I discovered them before they could do too much harm."

That calmed Doyle down considerably. "What do you expect of me? Hell, I got no wire or posts."

Lou could breathe a little easier. His father was listening to him.

"I know that, Pa," Lou said quietly. "But you can help me until I can get that fence repaired. You can make sure those cows are kept away from that break."

Doyle stared at him, his jaw going slack. "Are you suggesting I guard my own cows on my own place?"

"Something like that, Pa," Lou said evenly. "It'd sure give me a hand."

He watched his father struggle with this idea. There was never any telling how Doyle would react to something new.

"What good will that do?" Doyle asked. "You put in a new fence, and my cows go through it again. Show me what's gained."

"They won't go through it this time," Lou said positively. "I'll put in posts none of your cows can break or knock over."

Doyle's lips were pursed as he shook his head.

"Damn it, I will," Lou stated. "This time, I'll get my posts from the post rock country. It'll eliminate a source of headaches for both of us."

Lou couldn't believe it, but his father wasn't finding this idea too hard to swallow.

"How long do you figure it will take to get that new fence in?" Doyle asked.

Lou shrugged. That was hard to say. It depended upon so many intangible things. "A couple of days should do it."

"You mean I got to keep a guard on that damned fence that long?" Doyle howled.

"I'll be doing all the hard work," Lou said softly.

The fire faded in Doyle's eyes. "Kirby, Yocum," he yelled at his two men. "Ride out with Lou and keep those damned cows out of his corn. I'll send somebody out to relieve you later."

Doyle looked around, then asked, "Where's your horse?"

Lou grinned. "I walked over. It was quicker than going back to the barn and saddling up."

Doyle shook his head in disgust. "You're really a plowman, aren't you? Kirby, give him a lift." He turned and stalked away.

Lou waited until the two men saddled, then mounted behind Kirby.

The horse gave a tentative buck, and Kirby sawed on the reins until the animal quieted down. "Like a lot of old men I know," Kirby observed. "He don't take kindly to any new ideas."

Kirby had been with Doyle for many years. His face was a sun-hardened piece of leather.

Lou grinned behind Kirby's back. "Think Doyle's getting soft, Andy?"

"He listened to you, didn't he? I can remember the time when he'd take a shot at a farmer for even daring to speak to him."

"Hell," Lou said. "There were many times when I didn't dare speak to him before I was a farmer."

"He's been one tough old boy," Kirby said reflectively. He added in quick loyalty to his boss, "I guess he's had to be. He's known some rough times."

"Who hasn't?" Lou replied. That wasn't because he didn't have a sympathy for Doyle; he was just being honest.

Nalley's face brightened as he saw the approach of the three riders.

Lou jumped to the ground and said, "Thanks, Andy," then asked Nalley, "Did the cows come back?"

"It's still in their heads. They wandered over here a couple of times. I swear they looked plumb disappointed when they saw me standing here."

"Probably. Sam, you know Kirby and Yocum?"

Nalley knew them, but there was a stiffness in his nod. Their paths hadn't had any reason to touch.

"Pa sent Andy and Bill out here to guard this break until I can get in a new fence." He looked at the two riders again. "Boys, I appreciate this."

Yocum shrugged with complete indifference. "It don't make any difference what we're doing. The old man buys twenty-four hours a day."

Lou nodded again, then walked away with Nalley.

"How did Doyle take it?" Nalley asked.

"He kinda surprised me," Lou admitted. "Didn't hardly raise a fuss at all. He sent those two out to guard the fence until I can get it repaired."

"Well, that's a change," Nalley said guardedly. "Him helping out a farmer."

Lou didn't let his grin show. He knew of one argument Doyle and Nalley had, and he suspected there were others. Doyle had never worked too hard at trying to make friends.

"Maybe he's mellowing, Sam."

Nalley didn't answer. He didn't have to let Lou know the doubt still remained with him.

Nalley squinted at the sky. "A big chunk of this day is already gone. We'll get a start early in the morning."

Lou arched his eyebrows. "We? Where are we going?" He was a little annoyed that Nalley apparently had forgotten all about the fence Lou had to put in.

Nalley chuckled at Lou's expression. "We're going after your posts. You've got neighbors. Every one of them owes you a little time. We'll meet at my house in the morning."

Lou started to protest, and Nalley drawled, "That's what neighbors are for, isn't it? A man would be in sorry shape, if he thought he couldn't call on his neighbors." He thought he saw unhappiness in Lou's face. "If you're a little skittish about asking them, I'll do it. I'm thick-skinned. I'll see you early tomorrow."

Lou's face worked. "Sam, I'll never be able to tell you how grateful I am."

"Horse shit," Nalley said placidly. "I've got a lot of your sweat in my place. Oh, oh," he said suddenly and stopped. He pointed at Lou's porch. "You've got a visitor."

Lou knew the horse tethered out before the porch too well. Oh Jesus Christ, he thought mournfully. Parnell didn't lose any time in going to Briner.

Briner was seated on the porch in Lou's favorite rocker, and he nodded to Lou and Nalley.

Lou's face was blank, but Nalley grinned as he asked, "Which one of us you after, Will?"

"You got a guilty conscience?" Briner drawled.

"Funny thing about a badge. Just seeing it brings out the guilt in a man," Nalley replied.

Briner chuckled in appreciation. "I want a few words with Lou."

"Then I guess I'll be going," Nalley said. He couldn't hide his anxiety as he looked at Lou. The anxiety said he wished he could do something for Lou.

Briner never ceased his rhythmic rocking as he watched Nalley mount and ride away.

"What brings you out here?" Lou asked. That was a false question, and it showed in his tone. He knew why Briner was out here.

Briner had a long series of terms in office. He did a competent job, and the voters appreciated that. He wasn't much bigger than Lou, and his eyes were placid enough, but they could turn colder than a blizzard.

Briner spat over the porch's edge. "Hear you were raising a little hell last night, Lou."

Lou felt his cheeks heating up. "I knew he'd run to you," he snapped.

"Don't you go getting feisty on me," Briner warned.

"Sorry, Will," Lou apologized. "I didn't have any intention of hitting Welles. It just happened. He said something I couldn't take."

"So I heard," Briner said dryly. "What are we going to do about this, Lou?"

Lou sat down in the swing, adding the creaking of its chains to Briner's rhythmic rocking. His hands dangled between his knees.

"Will, you know I don't go around making trouble," Lou said earnestly.

"That's why we're just talking about it, Lou," Briner said.

That put a renewed hope in Lou. Briner wasn't out here to act tough. He grinned wanly at the sheriff. "I can promise you it won't happen again."

"It better hadn't, Lou. Welles will scream his head off when he learns I'm not doing anything about it. He was way out of line." He bobbed his head at the question in Lou's face. "Sure, I talked to three of the men who saw and heard everything. They all said the same thing. I didn't have to question the others. What I'm worried about, Lou, is will it happen again?" He paused as though trying to decide whether to plunge in deeper. "Everybody's talking about you seeing Celia, Lou."

"My business," Lou flared.

"Sure," Briner conceded. "Unless somebody else wants to comment about it. Are you going to try to shut their fat mouths the same way?"

"If you think I might run into trouble with Sam Nalley, you can forget it. He understands."

Briner nodded. "I saw you two together." His further curiosity showed in his eyes, but he didn't put it into words. "What I'm trying to tell you is that people are going to talk, and another nasty remark can set you off again."

Lou shook his head. "They won't bother me. You can depend on that."

"I hope so," Briner warned. A grin moved that leathery face. "We can't have you going around assaulting our most illustrious citizens, can we?" His eyes danced with mirth. "You did a pretty good job on Welles. His nose looked like a growing pumpkin this morning." Briner's face sobered, and he pointed at Lou. "Don't make me come out here again."

That was sound advice, and Lou didn't resent it. "You've got my word, Will."

"Good," Briner said and stood. "How are the crops looking this year?"

"Never had better prospects, Will," Lou said. "If things turn out the way they look, I'll more than make up for last year."

"Glad to hear that," Briner replied. "This country could stand a little good luck. Be seeing you."

"Sure," Lou said. "But not under the same circumstances."

Briner chuckled, stood, and walked toward his horse.

Lou watched him until he was out of sight. Briner's advice still rang in his mind. Briner stated it pretty plainly: keep your head, or you'll wind up in serious trouble.

Lou frowned as a thought struck him. What if trouble happened between him and Herrick when he tried to talk to him about the cornfield. Oh damn it, Lou thought sorrowfully. Briner wouldn't appreciate new trouble breaking out so soon on the heels of last night. That familiar stubborn set was in Lou's face again. He was going to say his piece to Herrick regardless of how Herrick took it or what happened afterward.

CHAPTER SEVEN

Lou arrived in town earlier than he ordinarily would have, but he wanted to talk to Cal Stricker before he walked into Storhmier's. To the best of his knowledge, Herrick didn't own a horse. If he wanted to ride any place, he must rent one. If Stricker said Herrick had rented a horse this morning, then Lou would have a pretty solid basis from which to accuse Herrick.

He swung down as Stricker approached him. "Good evening, Cal."

Stricker's eyes were fixed covetously on Dandy. "It would be, if I owned him."

Lou's laugh showed his pleasure. "You belong to a long list of men who want him, Cal."

"Not hard to believe, Lou. What can I do for you? I know you don't want another horse. Not with him."

"Cal, do you know Phil Herrick?"

"Storhmier's floorman? Sure. He comes in occasionally to rent a horse. In fact, he rented one this morning." His eyes shone with a memory of the morning. "We had a few unpleasant words, and I gave him Caesar to learn him a lesson. I'll tell you one thing. Herrick's a rider. He tamed Caesar down in a hurry. That one's been around a lot of horses."

Lou had all the information he needed. Herrick was out this morning. Lou was more positive than ever he had seen Herrick ride by.

As Lou started to mount, Stricker cried, "Is that all you came in for? To ask a question about Herrick?"

"You don't know how much it did for me," Lou said gravely. "I appreciate it, Cal." He waved to Stricker and rode out of the runway.

All right, he reasoned on his way to Storhmier's. You learned something. What are you going to do with it? He shook his head as he swung down before Storhmier's. He didn't know yet. But he was sure going to say something to Herrick. What happened after that was up to Herrick.

The tie rack was empty. This was earlier than the usual rush. That was all to the good. Lou would have every opportunity to talk to Herrick and Celia, but not together. He wanted to talk to Celia first.

His face fell as he saw Celia and Herrick seated at the same table. They must be enjoying themselves, for as Lou watched, Celia threw back her head and laughed at something Herrick said.

Lou didn't realize he was frowning. He didn't want to talk to Herrick until he asked Celia some questions. He might not be able to manage this the way he wanted.

He marched up to the table, his face frozen.

Herrick looked up at him and groaned in mock distress. "You again? Seems like some things you can't get rid of."

Lou looked steadily at Herrick. That could be a wariness in Herrick's eyes.

All right, Lou thought. Maybe it would be best to say what he wanted before Celia.

"I want to talk to you, Herrick," he said harshly.

"Go ahead," Herrick said. "You haven't got anything to say that I don't want Celia to hear."

"Maybe I have," Lou said grimly. "You ruined a lot of my corn this morning."

Herrick's eyes widened, and his mouth went momentarily slack. "Listen to the farmer," he jeered. "Sometimes, I think working out in all that sun addles their brains." He glanced at Celia, inviting her to enjoy his humor.

Lou thought Celia's breathing quickened, but he didn't look at her. "You were out to my place, Herrick, this morning."

Now, he was sure there was a definite catch in Herrick's breathing. "Don't deny it," Lou said savagely. "I saw you. You rented a horse from Stricker. I checked with him just a few minutes ago."

Mock helplessness spread over Herrick's face. "I told you he was sunstruck," he said to Celia.

"And you're a damned liar," Lou said furiously. "You tore down some of my fence and let Pa's cattle into my corn. I was lucky enough to be out at that field and saw them. They didn't do nearly as much damage as you hoped for."

"Who are you calling a liar?" Herrick blustered. His cheekbones seemed to stand out more prominently. He stood and roared, "Goddamn it. I don't take that from anybody."

Herrick's reaction satisfied Lou. Maybe he couldn't actually prove what Herrick did, but he knew.

"You just did," Lou snapped. "I'm warning you, if I ever see you on my place again, I'll blow your head off."

The startled flash in Herrick's eyes told Lou that the warning hit him hard. Maybe it was enough to hold Herrick back from another attempt at mischief. If it wasn't, Lou meant exactly what he said.

Herrick's breathing was a ragged, tearing sound. "Why, damn you," he raged. "I'll shut your mouth in a hurry."

Lou braced himself as Herrick started around the table. A worried thought flashed across his mind, but Herrick wasn't responsible for it. Oh Lord, he thought. If Briner hears about a brawl in here, he's going to raise pure hell.

Lou felt no personal concern. Herrick was bigger, but Lou thought he was soft. Indoor work such as Herrick knew didn't do much to harden his muscles.

"Here now, Phil," a voice interrupted Herrick's movement. "Take it easy."

Lou flashed a glance at Storhmier. Despite Storhmier's bulk he moved with surprising lightness. He had moved so softly that Lou didn't know he was anywhere around until Storhmier spoke. He was a grossly fat man, the excess weight showing the extent of his good living.

"What's this all about?" Storhmier asked mildly.

"He called me a liar," Herrick said furiously. "I'm going to knock his damned head off."

Storhmier held up a fat hand, checking Herrick's forward surge. He squinted at Lou. "That true, Lou?"

Herrick was like a sorely badgered animal, needing violence to ease the pressure that squeezed him so badly. Lou had the upper hand now and knew it. He felt oddly calm and relaxed. There wasn't any physical attractiveness in Storhmier's appearance, but in his few dealings with Storhmier, Lou had found him to be a fair man.

"It's true, Quincy," Lou said steadily. "He did some damage to my corn. Look at him! Doesn't that prove it?"

Storhmier turned his head to scrutinize Herrick's face. Herrick was oddly pale, and twin patches of red stood out against the stark background. His mouth opened and closed, but he made no sound.

"He sure looks guilty," Storhmier said speculatively.

Storhmier's backing Lou enraged Herrick, and he found his voice.

"Why should I want to do that? Nothing that hick does could interest me."

Storhmier looked at Celia, then at Herrick. "Keep on, Phil. You're proving what he said. Lou has caused me no trouble. He pays for what he orders. Why don't you move along, Phil, and let him alone?"

Herrick's eyes were murderous, but they couldn't stand up against Storhmier's level stare. He whirled and rushed away. The weight of his anger showed in the hard slam of his heels against the floor.

Storhmier chuckled. He had enjoyed the whole byplay. Phil had been getting more and more cocky. It was about time somebody cut him down to more sizable proportions.

"That suit you, Lou?" he asked.

"I want to talk to Celia," Lou answered.

"I don't see anybody stopping you," Storhmier said and waddled away.

Celia was furious as Lou sat down across the table from her. It showed in her too rapid breathing, the way her bosom heaved, and the glint in her eyes.

"Why did you jump all over Phil like that?" she demanded.

Her attack astounded Lou, and he barely refrained from snapping back at her. "You heard what I told him," he said coldly.

"But you had no proof," she cried.

"You saw his face," Lou said. He was getting angrier by the second. "That should have convinced you." He thought of what he could have lost this morning, and he shook inwardly. "I think you might have caused all this, Celia."

That startled and infuriated her. "Now, you're trying to blame me, and I don't even know what you're talking about."

Lou doggedly shook his head. This was getting out of hand, and he hadn't intended it to turn that way. But he had to know if Celia said anything to Herrick about the corn. He needed it for his own satisfaction.

"Did you say anything to Herrick about my corn?"

Celia couldn't meet Lou's probing stare. "Why should I? Do you think everybody is interested in what you're doing?"

She did say something to Herrick, Lou knew with a certainty. He didn't believe she had set out to do him definite harm, but she had talked about him to Herrick. Lou could see how it might have happened. In her enthusiasm she had mentioned Lou's prospects, and that was enough to plant a poisonous seed in Herrick's mind.

Lou stared miserably at her. None of that mattered now. His desire for her was as strong as ever, and here they sat quarreling.

"I didn't want this night to turn out this way, Celia," he said slowly.

Some of the defiance still remained in her face, but she said, "Neither did I, Lou. It's happened too quick. Neither of us knows the other." She remembered something Herrick said to her. "Don't you see? We live in two different worlds."

That scared him. He could lose her right now. "It's all my fault. I came in here hotheaded. I wasn't accusing you. I was only trying to find out how it happened. Nothing's changed, Celia. The thought of losing what I promised you scared me. That's all."

He reached out and captured one of her hands, but she didn't return his pressure.

Lou smiled with a confidence he didn't feel. "I rushed you too hard, Celia. What I told you still stands. All you need is more time to think about it."

She tried to smile at him. "Maybe that's it, Lou. But you came in here looking so mean. You frightened me."

Lou acknowledged that with a grave nod. "I can see that, Celia." He was wise enough not to press her further tonight. "Will you just think about it some more? That's all I'm asking."

The full strength of her smile returned; it was that smile that had captured him in the first place. "Oh yes, Lou," she breathed. "You'll come back?"

He stood and said, "You know it, Celia. I'll be back just as soon as I can."

Lou looked at her for a long moment before he nodded and turned away from the table. He passed Herrick on the way out. He met Herrick's glowering with cold, steady eyes. Just say one word to me, Lou begged. But Herrick turned away without opening his mouth.

Lou walked out, untied Dandy, and mounted. He was scared deep down inside. The chance he could lose Celia was only a part of the problem, but other disturbing elements remained. He couldn't forget the way she flew to Herrick's defense. Of course, she hadn't understood what was behind Lou's attack on Herrick. Lou tried to strengthen that excuse all the way home.

CHAPTER EIGHT

Six men were sitting on Nalley's porch when Lou arrived in the morning. Nalley had hitched up too, and six wagons were in the yard. Lou's wagon made the seventh. They could accomplish a lot of work with that many wagons.

Lou stopped his wagon behind the others. His needed tools were in the wagon bed. He didn't relish the prospects ahead. It was going to be a long and brutal day, and that wouldn't finish the job.

Lou wasn't in the best of moods this morning. He hadn't slept well, spending most of the night staring at the blackened ceiling. Celia had said something about them living in different worlds. Could those two worlds be joined and both of them find happiness in it? The elusiveness of the answer to that question was what bothered Lou. He wasn't backing out; he had asked a woman to marry him, and he still wanted her. Then why did all these little doubts keep creeping in? Lou couldn't answer that, either.

The men greeted Lou boisterously as he climbed down from the wagon and approached the porch.

"I knew better than to agree to come today," Riley said, "when Nalley approached me yesterday. I've been around him long enough to know when he comes around, you're going to get sucked into work."

The soberness of Lou's face didn't crack, even though he knew Riley was only joshing him. "I'll never be able to tell you how much I appreciate this. I'll pay all of you back."

Nabor made a rude noise, then he saw Lou was serious. "Aw, cut it out, Lou. I think every man here owes you more than this little bit of work. I remember you putting in quite a bit of time a couple of years ago when I needed a barn. If we go down the list, every man here could remember something you've done for them. Hell, that's what neighbors are for. All of us would be in sorry shape, if we didn't give the other a hand."

Heads bobbed in solemn agreement.

"Sam tells me you could've lost a lot of corn," Mellinger said. A shudder ran through him. "All of us are thinking of the same thing happening to us."

Their faces told Lou he would be only flogging a dead horse, if he attempted to say more about the matter.

"Anyway, I appreciate what you told Briner. He was out to see me."

"You mean about your set-to with Welles?" Westhoff asked. At Lou's nod, he went on. "We only told him what happened. Briner cause you any trouble, Lou?"

Lou managed a faint grin. "He warned me I couldn't go around hitting influential citizens because I didn't like what they said."

That released general laughter. "I just hope you never have to try to borrow money from Welles," Westhoff commented.

"Me too," Lou said with feeling.

"You eat breakfast, Lou?" Nalley asked.

"I wasn't hungry," Lou replied. Before he could add more, Nalley raised his voice and called, "Maude, bring Lou some of that coffeecake you baked this morning."

Lou wanted to refuse. He was still embarrassed by the stiff words between him and Maude the other evening, but if he said no, he would only make a point of it.

Maude came out with a plate of several slices of coffeecake and a cup of steaming coffee.

Despite Lou's statement he wasn't hungry, the aroma of the freshly baked cake filled his nostrils and aroused a rumble in his belly. Memory was his final undoing. He had eaten other things Maude had baked.

"Good morning, Lou." Maude said it easily enough, but her usual smile was missing.

Lou bit into a slice of the cake and said, "Good, Maude," without looking directly at her. He was sorry about the rift between them, but he didn't feel as though it was all his fault.

"I'm glad you like it." Maude offered the plate again.

Lou wanted to refuse, but the taste of the cake wouldn't let him. "Well, maybe another piece." He took another bite and washed it down with a swallow of the excellent coffee. Maude was just a good all-around cook.

Maude turned and went back into the house. If the coolness between her and Lou was noticed, nobody commented on it.

"Maude fixed some sandwiches," Nalley said. "I'll get them. Everybody ready?"

Assorted groans greeted that question. "As ready as we'll ever be," Mellinger answered. "Lou, how many posts do you figure we need?"

"I know there's twenty broken posts," Lou replied. He wanted so badly to say he'd like to replace other weak posts, but that would be pushing too hard.

Mellinger nodded after a moment of thought. "We'd better double that number. There could be other weak posts. While we're at it, we might as well do a thorough job."

Heads bobbed agreement. Lou could have kissed every one of them.

"Let's get at it," Mellinger said. He threw an arm across Lou's shoulders as they walked toward the wagons. "It's not the work anybody's objecting to. It's just accepting the fact that it has to be done."

"That's the truth," Lou said and grinned.

The limestone quarry was six miles from Lou's place. Lou knew it well. The limestone outcropped in layers six to eight inches thick. Widths of those layers could be drilled and wedged off to make enduring posts. Once one of those posts was put into a fence line, a man could forget about replacing it in his lifetime. Lou had often vowed he was going to put in some of his fence with those posts, but he never found the time. Other jobs kept popping up, and the placement of the stone posts had to be put off. It took an emergency, such as this, to force a man into the necessary hard work.

Post rock country extended over seventeen counties in North Central Kansas. Russell sat about in the heart of that area.

The wagons pulled up to the quarry and stopped. Men climbed down and stood for a few moments, gloomily surveying the outcroppings. Nabor pulled on a pair of heavy gloves. "I wish it was over." He laughed as a thought amused him. "Why hasn't somebody harnessed wishes. If you could, you might be able to get a lot of work done with them."

Lou echoed Nabor's laugh. "Work on it, boy. Maybe you can get a patent on that idea."

" 'Fraid not," Nabor said. He lifted his hands. "I haven't found a substitute for these yet."

Lou pulled on his own gloves, picked up a drill, and started on the first hole, setting the bit some eight inches away from the edge of the rock. He cranked away, grinning as he thought of what Nabor said.

The bit cut easily into the relatively soft rock. Behind Lou, the others drilled similar holes, keeping on the line Lou started. When the post was finally broken free, it would be some eight inches square and about six feet long. If the post was cut thinner, it would shatter or crack. At this width, the post would be brutally heavy, weighing from two hundred and fifty to five hundred pounds.

Lou drilled his hole to the depth he wanted and straightened. He looked back along the line. Tilden and Riley weren't quite finished with their drilling, and Mellinger said, "What happened to you two? You must have hit a knothole."

Tilden grinned at him. "I always get the toughest hole."

When the holes were drilled, wedges were inserted in the line of holes. Each wedge was tapped simultaneously until the post cracked off.

Tilden joined him. "That looks like a four-and-one post."

At Lou's questioning look, Tilden explained. "It'll take four men and a boy to get this one in a wagon. But if we ever get it planted in the ground, it'll never come out."

"That's the kind I'm looking for," Lou said.

They went back to work, drilling their holes, then tapping the wedges to force a fissure along the selected line. Each post split off with a sharp little crack. This wasn't too hard; the really hard work would come when those posts had to be lifted and placed in the wagons.

Lou counted the posts after several hours of work. He was pleasantly surprised to see how many lay in a long rough line. It was going better than he hoped for. They should have their forty posts before the day was out.

Nalley squinted at the sun. "It's past noon. How about lunch?"

Lou willingly dropped his tools and walked over to Nalley's wagon. He sat down and put his back against a wagonwheel. He was tired, but his muscles weren't screaming at him yet.

Nalley opened a large, brown bag and handed out the sandwiches. "All I brought along is water," he apologized.

Westhoff took a huge bite of his sandwich, then washed it down with a long swig of water from the canteen.

"Still the best drink ever made," he observed.

Riley shook his head in disagreement. "I can name one that's better." He smacked his lips in memory. "Irish whiskey."

"You must have a cast-iron gut," Nabor said caustically. "The only time I drank Irish whiskey, I couldn't raise my head for three days."

"Then it wasn't properly aged," Riley stated. "Good Irish whiskey is mellow along with its kick. Ain't that right, Lou?"

Lou shook his head as he reached for the canteen. "You're asking the wrong man. I never drank any Irish whiskey that I know of. I'll stick to this." He sloshed the water around in the canteen. "I've got work to do. I never found the time when whiskey and work went very well together."

"Your education has been neglected," Riley said sadly.

Lou finished his sandwich and said, "Good sandwich, Sam."

"You can thank Maude for that," Nalley said.

Lou knew that. He nodded without speaking. One sandwich was all Lou wanted. Several of the others had their second sandwich. This kind of capacity for food always awed Lou. He guessed by the others' standards, he would be called a poor eater.

He stretched out on the ground, cushioning his head in his locked hands. He didn't intend to go to sleep, but a shoe prodded him into wakefulness.

"You gonna sleep the whole afternoon?" Nabor asked.

"Just waiting for the rest of you to finish stuffing your guts," Lou said and sat up. He yawned and stretched. Just those few minutes had refreshed him. "Let's get the rest of them."

Lou stopped drilling in midafternoon and came over to Nalley. "That makes it, Sam."

Now, the really brutal work would start. If Lou thought he was tired now, just wait until those wagons were loaded.

They distributed the forty posts among the seven wagons, judiciously watching the weight. Five of those big brutes would weigh a ton, or more. The horses could pull that much weight, but a wagon could be broken down. It took four men to lift some of the heavier posts and slide them into the wagon bed. Tilden was right when he said it would take four men and a boy to handle this kind of weight.

Lou climbed onto his wagon, and the others let him take the lead. Lou slumped in his seat as he drove. This day was beginning to take a lot out of him. He wanted these posts on the inside of the wire to bulwark the wire against any future pressure the cows might put on the fence.

He was surprised to see Doyle with Kirby and Yocum when he drove to the end of his cornfield. Was Doyle out here to rush the job along? Hell, Lou thought with quick indignation. He told Doyle he'd get the job done in a couple of days. He was ahead of schedule.

He pulled up and stopped, and Doyle rode over to him. "Moved along pretty fast," Doyle commented.

That was a change. It was rare Doyle offered a complimentary word. "The other wagons are right behind me," Lou said. "I'm waiting for them to help me unload."

Doyle swung down. "No use waiting for them. The two of us can do it."

"Why sure," Lou agreed, but a wicked gleam danced in his eyes. Doyle was contemptuous, particularly of what another man was doing. Maybe this would change his thinking a little.

"We'll just slide a post out and let it fall," Lou said. "Then I'll drive up a few feet to unload the next one. There's no sense carrying these things even an extra foot."

Doyle reached for one of the posts, and Lou waited for his reaction.

Doyle strained and tugged, his face growing redder. "Jesus Christ," he exploded. "These damned things must be made out of lead."

"Just about," Lou said and chuckled. His father never had any respect for farmers. This should do a lot to change that opinion.

"You just going to stand there, or are you going to give me a hand?" Doyle yelled.

"Thought you could handle it by yourself, Pa," Lou said sober-faced. He better help his father before he popped a gut.

Their combined efforts slid the post a grudging inch at a time along the wagon bed. Finally, enough of the post protruded from the wagon to overbalance it. It toppled to the ground, falling with a heavy thud.

Sweat ran down Doyle's face, and he leaned against the wagon to catch his breath. "My God," he gasped. "You been handling these things all day?"

The irascible bite was gone from his voice. Lou knew better than to grin. This should give his father a little taste of what a farmer was up against.

Lou looked around at the rumble of wheels. "Here come the others," he announced. "There's enough help so that we don't have to pull out our insides."

"You mean you got six more wagons?" Doyle asked. His relief at the arrival of more help was evident in his voice.

"You see them, Pa," Lou said quietly.

"That's enough to put in a whole line," Doyle exploded.

"Just the break, Pa. Maybe a few more to replace the rottenest posts."

The others drove up. Every man knew Doyle, but there was no open cordiality in their manner, nor any attempt to shake hands. The old animosity between farmer and rancher still existed.

"We just started unloading," Lou said to Nalley. He couldn't resist a few malicious words. "A rancher's not used to handling this kind of weight."

Nalley nodded slowly. "Pretty heavy, ain't they, Mr. Manard? Too heavy for just the two of you."

Lou couldn't believe it, but Doyle said, "Too damned heavy for me. I about pulled out a gut."

Just let it lay, Sam, Lou begged. This was the first giving in of any kind he had ever known in Doyle.

"Sure," Nalley said, and there was no derision in the word. He called, "Tilden, Riley, Nabor. You want to give me a hand with this wagon?" He glanced at Lou. "Drive the wagon, Lou." He forestalled Lou's objection by adding, "Save us a lot of time, if you just drive instead of climbing off and on."

Lou grinned. He could forget about trying further to impress Doyle. He'd already proven he could handle these posts. "Right, Sam," he said and climbed back up on the seat.

Lou drove along, pausing every ten feet to unload another post. With men working together, it didn't take long to strip the load off the wagon. Lou wondered if Doyle had learned anything from that.

Lou walked the fence line, looking closely at every post. Every now and then, he leaned his weight onto a post to test it. He decided he needed a dozen replacements.

He walked back to Tilden's wagon, the last waiting to be unloaded. "Eight posts too many, Hank," he said. "Can you use them?"

"Hell, yes," Tilden said eagerly.

"Just leave them on," Lou said.

He set about digging the postholes. Thank God, he found no rock in this land, and the holes dug easily. The entire job wouldn't be done by nightfall, but they'd chew up a big bite out of the chore.

The holes were dug ten feet apart, and Nabor and Westhoff helped him lift one end of the first post enough so that the other end could be slid into the hole. Lou tested the post after the dirt was shoveled back and tamped. He couldn't budge it.

Doyle came over and tested the post. "That's strong enough to hold an elephant," he grunted.

"Maybe you oughta go into raising elephants," Nabor said slyly.

Doyle wasn't known for his sense of humor, and Lou held his breath, waiting for the explosion.

"Maybe you got an idea at that," Doyle said and grinned. "You show me a market for them, and I'll consider it."

Lou couldn't believe it, but his father was mellowing.

Other men worked ahead, digging the postholes, and Lou, Nabor and Westhoff moved to slide the second post into the freshly dug hole.

Doyle pursed his lips and said, "Putting those posts in awful close, ain't you? Looks like you intend building a solid wall."

"A little closer spaced than usual," Lou acknowledged. "But this is one stretch of fence we want to be certain will never cause any more trouble."

Doyle looked skeptical, but he didn't argue. "Think you'll have it done tomorrow?"

"Should," Lou answered. The work was going faster than he hoped.

Half of the downed posts were replaced when Lou looked at Nalley and said, "Be dark before you get home, Sam. How about calling it a day?"

Nalley rolled his heavy shoulders to ease the ache in them. "Suits me. I'm sure the others will agree."

Lou heard no disagreement from any of the others.

"If you'll guard the break one more night, Pa," Lou said to Doyle, "then it'll be over."

"A hell of a lot faster than I expected," Doyle replied. He looked reflectively at Lou's bunch of men.

"I'll say one thing, Lou. They know what they're doing."

"Good men," Lou said quietly. "Good night, Pa."

"One other thing," Doyle said, stopping Lou. "Figure out how much damage you think this has cost you. I'll settle up."

This was another change. Not too far back, an incident like this would have aroused violent tempers, and men could have been hurt. Maybe Doyle was beginning to see the other man's side.

"Not enough damage to bother with, Pa." Besides, it wasn't his father's blame. Herrick was responsible for all this trouble, and Lou knew how far he would get trying to get damages out of Herrick.

He nodded to his father and walked toward his wagon. Nalley waited for him there.

"We made good time, Sam," Lou said. "I'll bring out new wire in the morning."

"We could untangle some of the old wire," Nalley objected.

Lou shook his head. "I've got the wire. I want to start out brand-new. I think a cow can see new wire better than old wire. Those cows are going to test this stretch again."

"It might be wiser," Nalley replied. "How about coming over to the house for supper?"

The invitation was tempting, and for a moment, Lou considered it. Then he shook his head. Maude might not show it, but she wouldn't be pleased at his presence.

"I'll pass it this time, Sam," he said gently. "I've got chores to do, then I just want to go to bed. See you in the morning."

Nalley didn't press it further, but he looked mournful. He was still standing there when Lou drove off.

Ordinarily, Lou would have been eager to get cleaned up and drive into town to see Celia. He wasn't lying when he said he was tired. But something else held him back. Was it fear that Celia would say yes? Lou examined the new thought with astonishment. Last night's argument had put a vast new change in him. He could see how far apart they were. Maybe the distance between them could never be closed. Did he still want her?

Lou avoided answering that question now. He was too weary to think further.

CHAPTER NINE

Lou plucked at the strand of tightened barbed wire with a forefinger, and it twanged reassuringly. That should be tight enough to suit anybody. This was the last strand. Lou couldn't be more satisfied that the fence was done, or practically so. Short pieces of wire would have to be snipped off, one end tied around the barbed wire, wrapped around the post, then secured on the other side of the post. That would hold the strands in proper spacing on the posts.

Lou pulled off a glove and sucked at a wire cut on his wrist. No matter how carefully he tried to protect himself, barbed wire was like a rattlesnake, biting when a man least expected it.

Nalley straightened from tying a strand in place. "Nothing prettier than a new fence, is there?"

"Sure isn't," Lou agreed.

Tilden came up and said, "Good job, Lou. With these stone posts in this line, you've strengthened this fence immeasurably. I don't think you have to worry for a while over this fence."

"I'm grateful to you," Lou said. "I'm in your debt."

Tilden grinned at Nalley. "Do you know what he's talking about?"

"Can't understand a word," Nalley replied.

Tilden turned his head and squinted. "Your pa's coming, Lou. He's sure been interested in this fence."

Lou nodded. "He'll be glad to know it's done. Saves some of his hands from riding this fence."

Tilden looked as though he wanted to say something but was afraid to.

"Go ahead," Lou invited.

"He's not the tough old bastard—" Tilden broke off and colored.

"He's been called that before," Lou said dryly.

Tilden chuckled. "Old bastard that I thought he was," he finished.

Doyle rode up to them and said, "Lou, call everybody over." He swung down and untied a demijohn from the horn of his saddle. "I figured finishing this fence called for some kind of a celebration."

Mellinger took the first drink and said solemnly, "Good whiskey."

Riley was next, and he didn't quite agree with Mellinger. "Not as good as Irish whiskey," he said stubbornly. "But damned good."

Maybe this was the way all fences should be celebrated, Lou thought, with a whiskey bottle passed back and forth over it.

He refused the demijohn the third time it was passed around. "Two drinks is all I can handle."

"He never was much of a drinking man," Doyle said.

Lou examined the remark to see if there was a caustic bite in it, then let it go. Maybe suspicion was the basis of all the trouble between him and his father.

"Maybe not," Nalley said and smiled. "But I'll tell you one thing. He's one hell of a good farmer."

Lou didn't dare look at his father, afraid to see affront on his face. Nalley's praise of Lou might rub Doyle the wrong way.

"Seems to be doing all right," Doyle said mildly. "Or maybe it's because of all you people picking him up."

Grins broke out on the assembled faces. My God, Lou thought. Doyle's human. Maybe Lou hadn't dug deep enough to find it.

"You all can stay here and empty the jug," Lou said. "But there's still a good piece of the day left. I've got corn that needs cultivating."

That aroused a clamor of protest, all of them urging Lou to stay.

"Aw, Lou," Tilden said. "You can get at it tomorrow. All of us can do some catching up then."

Lou firmly shook his head. "I can get some of it done before night. Be seeing you, Pa."

"You'll be over again?" Doyle asked.

For a moment their eyes met, and Lou could swear there was a plea in the older man's eyes. Momentarily, Lou was filled with rebellion. Not once had his father been over to see him. That road ran two ways. It was no longer for Lou than it was for Doyle. He pushed the childish rebellion aside. With sudden clarity, Lou realized if there was to be any relationship between them, he would have to make the moves. It was odd that with his acceptance of that thought, all his resentment vanished.

"You know it, Pa," he said easily. He nodded to the rest of the men and walked toward his wagon, feeling a new warmth inside. For the first time he could remember in a long while, the two Manards had spent some time together without lashing out at each other.

Lou drove home and unhitched the team, leaving Buster harnessed. "More work, Buster," he said and grinned. "Don't look so sorrowful. It's Molly's time to rest. She did the last cultivating, didn't she?"

He hitched Buster to the cultivator and drove back to the cornfield. The corn had been cultivated twice, but in just the short time since the last cultivating, the weeds had sprung up all over. Weeds must be sent by the devil, for they seemed to have a fiendish intelligence of their own. Cut them down one week, and in a few days they were in full growth. It was too bad that man hadn't learned to make a living off them, for weeds thrived without care. Even a drought didn't seem to intimidate weeds, and just a little rain made them thrive.

Lou smiled at his thoughts. If this was criticism of his maker, he apologized. But it did seem that things could be made a little easier for farmers.

His apology didn't make him feel any kinder toward the weeds. "Damned things," he grumbled as he started down a corn row. This would probably be the last time over this field, for in another week, the corn would be too high to cultivate without breaking down the stalks.

Lou knew a savage delight as the shovels turned over the soil. What weeds weren't rooted out were smothered under the blanket of freshly turned earth. He should be done with this field in three or four days.

Despite how much he tried thoughts of Celia kept creeping into his mind. This cornfield was part of the prospects he had spoken of to her the other night. He hadn't lied to her; he couldn't remember seeing his corn look any better at this stage. It could have all been wiped out, he thought in sudden anger. Did he still blame Celia for putting an idea in Herrick's head? Lou was afraid he did. Her reaction upset him the most. Instead of showing genuine concern, she had flared at him. Two different worlds! The phrase kept running through Lou's mind.

I wasn't lying to her, Lou thought. This is going to be a good year. He thought of the twenty-five head of steers he had purchased at the beginning of spring. They would fatten on the good grass in the south pasture and gain weight. That would bring additional profit. It hit him with a sudden clarity that those things were only figures, having no real meaning to Celia. Lou looked at them with entirely different eyes. Perhaps his proposal had been flattering, and the moment touched her. But so far, he aroused no desperate need in her. Would she ever feel that? It was another of the unanswered questions. Did he have the same need of her he first felt? Maybe it was beginning to weaken. He knew one thing for sure. He always had a tendency to rush into things. He was going to have to curb his impatience and learn to weigh things with his mind and not his heart. Sure, he was going to see Celia again. He wanted that. But from now on, he would let things develop naturally without insisting they be bent his way.

CHAPTER TEN

Lou greased the cultivator and put it away in the barn. He wouldn't need it again this year. The corn was laid by, and all he needed from now on was a little more co-operation from nature. If the rains came at the right time, he could look forward to a bumper crop.

He dipped out a bucketful of grain and walked about, scattering it for the chickens. He listened to the busy clucking of the hens as they rushed about, picking up the kernels. Lou couldn't say he had a great love for chickens, for they were stupid birds, but he owed them a solid vote of thanks. He got a lot of his living from these chickens. An egg was the quickest way Lou knew of to prepare a meal, and it was filling, though at times, he could barely stand to look at another one.

He turned his head at the rumble of wheels. Lou was always ready to welcome a visitor. Solitude was a fine thing and needed by everyone, but at times, it could become overwhelming.

Lou's face brightened as he saw Nalley climb down from his buggy.

Lou went out to greet him. "How's it going, Sam?"

"I'm afraid to say it," Nalley replied cautiously. "But things couldn't be going better. I just finished cultivating for the last time this year." He drew a deep breath. "I'm going to say it, even though it's defying the devil. I'm looking at what could be the finest year I ever had."

"Isn't that great?" Lou said with enthusiasm. "I hope everybody can say the same thing."

Nalley nodded. "They should be able to. Everything's been on our side. Even a lazy man can't help but make some crops."

Lou smiled. That wouldn't apply to Nalley or himself. Both of them were hard-working men, doing the things that needed to be done at the right time.

"I just finished too, Sam," Lou said. "For the first time, I'm all caught up. Of course, the barn and house need some repairs, and I should start painting the house." There was no criticism in his eyes as he looked at the house. It was a good house, solidly built to endure. He could thank Hiram for that. Lou loved the broad porch, shaded by the two great hard maple trees. He spent a lot of his evening hours out there. Hiram had shown a lot of wisdom in planting those maples in a treeless country. Lou didn't know how old those trees were, but Hiram must have been a very young man when he planted them.

"Did you ever know of a farmer who was completely caught up?" Nalley asked. "The only way he can get a rest is just to shut his eyes and sit down."

Lou nodded solemnly. He knew; he'd been there. But the subject of painting wasn't out of his mind. "Maybe I can get at the painting this fall."

"I've been thinking that the last four years," Nalley said. "Sarah's been on my back to get at it. She says we're looking pretty shabby. She's right." He grinned broadly. "But something always comes up and saves me. Like that piece of your fence. You should have heard her squawk when I said it had to be done first. Have you been back out there since we finished it, Lou?"

"Several times. A couple of times I found Pa's cows right up against the fence. They were looking longingly at my corn, but that was as far as they could go. Sam, I can't tell you how grateful—"

"Are you going to start that stuff again?" Nalley interrupted. "One of these days, I'm going to need some fencing myself."

"Good. Just let me know when you intend to start."

Nalley winked at Lou. "Wouldn't it be funny if starting on the fence hit on the same date Sarah picked for me to start at the painting?" His face sobered. "Lord, she'd peel hide off of me this wide." He held his hands eighteen inches apart.

Lou laughed. He was amused, though he envied Nalley. Nalley was a contented man. He had his home and family, and he didn't spend any lonely hours.

"How about a cup of coffee, Sam?"

"Your coffee?" Nalley said in derision. "I'm not that hard up."

"Go to hell," Lou retorted, but he wasn't ruffled. Both Sarah and Maude could turn out a far better cup of coffee than he could.

"How about you coming into town with me?" Nalley asked. "I've got to pay Parnell a gallon of my blood. Payment on the place is due," he explained. At the refusal forming on Lou's face, he said, "You said you were caught up."

"I'm not even cleaned up," Lou protested.

Nalley looked speculatively at him. "Boy, you've changed. You used to be so damned eager to get into town. Now, you're hunting excuses."

Lou's face colored. He didn't want Nalley thinking he was avoiding going into town. Besides, it was too early to expect to see Celia. He still wasn't ready to talk to her. Oh Lord, his thinking was really getting muddled.

"Maybe I should go into town, Sam," he said slowly. "I'm about out of everything. And I need a little cash. As long as you're going to the bank, I might as well go in too and draw out a few dollars."

"The blessed and the unblessed," Nalley said and sighed. At Lou's upraised eyebrows, Nalley explained, "You go in to draw out money. I go in to pay in money."

Lou grinned in good-natured acceptance. That was only due to Lou's mother and Hiram, but he didn't take time to explain. "It'll just take me a minute to change."

"Take all the time you want," Nalley replied.

Inside the house, Lou stripped off his soiled overalls and shirt. He donned a fresh pair of pants and a clean shirt. He looked with distaste at the garment's wrinkled condition. He was never much of a hand with an iron. He shrugged away his annoyance. At least, the shirt and pants were clean.

Nalley whistled when Lou joined him. "Hey, you're all dressed up. You make me feel like I should go back home and change."

"Sure, I'm a dude," Lou said lightly. He climbed into the buggy. The buggy was old, but this was still traveling in style. The buggy cushion was a lot softer than a wagon seat, or even a saddle. "I only got rid of the worst dirt," he continued. "If I hadn't, I'd be afraid Welles would bar me from his bank."

"Naw," Nalley disclaimed. "It's your money he's holding, isn't it?" He caught the twinkle in Lou's eyes and knew he was being kidded. He slapped the reins on the mare's rump. Like the buggy, she had some age on her, but she still stepped out smartly.

"Have you seen Welles since that night, Lou?" Nalley asked.

"I haven't had any reason to need money." Lou stretched luxuriously. He was glad Nalley had asked him to ride into town.

"Welles might give me a few hard looks," Lou went on. "But I don't expect anything more. Briner made it clear he wouldn't stand for any more foolishness between us." He grinned and added, "I believe him.

Briner can be one tough man." Lou was silent for a moment. "I wish Russell had another bank. I'd sure like to switch my account."

"Listen to him," Nalley said plaintively. "He's got so damned much money he worries about where to put it."

Lou snorted. "I wish that was true." He watched the scenery a moment longer. He couldn't remember when he had seen things so lush and green. The conviction grew within him. This was going to be a year to remember. Then why was he so scared of talking seriously to Celia again? They had one little quarrel, but that had been straightened out. By now, she had plenty of time to think over what he said. She should be wondering why Lou hadn't been back for his answer. He recalled how she looked the first time he saw her, and the eagerness came back. Everything was going to be all right between them. All he had to do was to believe it.

"Seen your pa since we finished the fence?" Nalley asked.

Lou glanced at Nalley. There was nothing sharp behind that question. "I haven't, Sam." There hadn't been any reason to, but he didn't say it.

"He's changed a lot, Lou," Nalley said reflectively. "He turned out to be right pleasant to be around. I don't mind admitting I was a little scared of him."

Lou could have echoed Nalley's statement. All that had changed. "We just worked on the same problem, Sam," he said quietly. "That made all the difference in the world. I hope Pa hits a good market this year," Lou said. "He can stand it."

"All you cattlemen talk that way," Nalley said. He laughed at Lou's expression. "Hell, you're a cattleman, too. I wish I'd had enough money to buy a few head myself last spring. Maybe next year—" His shrug finished for him. It said that he had to make a living first before he tried to make money.

"It's a struggle, Sam," Lou said. That stated it all. Lou hoped prosperity would come to every man struggling to wrest a living out of the land. Prosperity was an elusive thing. A man purely wore himself out, trying to discover where it was hiding.

They didn't say much the remainder of the trip into town. Nalley pulled up before the hitch rack in front of the bank. He grimaced and asked, "What was that machine called the Frenchmen used to cut off people's heads? I remember learning about it when I was in school."

"You mean a guillotine?"

"That's it. Here goes a man facing one."

Lou chuckled. "It's only money, Sam."

"That's all," Nalley said gloomily. "Well, this buys me another year's time."

Lou walked into the bank with Nalley. Only old Charley Mills was in the teller's cage. He had worked here for as long as Lou could remember, and all those years were beginning to lay their harsh, unrelenting tracks on him. His hair was snow white, and there was a perceptible trembling in his hands.

My God, Lou thought, appalled. Mills had spent most of his life working within these four walls. Lou wondered if Mills had had a raise in all that time. Knowing Parnell he doubted it, or if there had been one, it was meager at best. It must be hell to need a job for bare survival. His face was sober as he greeted Mills.

"How are you doing, Charley?"

Mills managed a wan grin. "Good enough for an old man I guess, Lou."

"Hell, Charley. You're going on forever. When I come in here fifty years from now, you'll still be behind this window."

Mills shuddered. "Oh God, I hope not. Surely, I haven't been bad enough to earn something like that."

Mills realized what he was saying and cast a fearful glance at the closed door behind his cage. He didn't have to say anything, but Lou knew Mills feared Parnell had overheard his remark.

Mills licked his lips and said hastily, "That was just a bad joke, Lou."

"Sure," Lou said easily. "Sam here has some business with Parnell. Is he in?"

The door in the rear of the room opened, and Parnell appeared in the doorway. "Charley," he bellowed. "I want to talk to you about the Jamison account."

Lou could swear Mills shriveled visibly. "Yes sir, Mr. Parnell. Mr. Nalley is here. He wants to see you."

Parnell greeted Nalley with a false affability, but his eyes were poisonous as they swept over Lou.

"Come in, come in, Mr. Nalley," he said.

Lou grinned sardonically. Sure, Parnell would greet Sam with open arms. He knew Nalley was here to make a payment.

Lou waited until the door closed behind Parnell and Nalley, then said, "Welles doesn't seem to be too fond of me."

"You shouldn't have hit him," Mills said reproachfully.

"So I've been told," Lou said dryly. Mills probably had only Parnell's version of the incident, and that would be colored strongly in Parnell's favor. Lou wasn't going to argue about it with Mills.

He handed over his passbook. "Charley, I want to withdraw twenty dollars."

Lou checked Mills's entry, not realizing he frowned as he did so.

"Something wrong, Lou?" Mills asked in instant alarm.

"Not of your doing," Lou said and smiled. "Anything I find wrong is of my doing. I'm just spending too damned much money." His account was a little under five hundred dollars. That wasn't being rich, but it wasn't poor, either. A farmer's paydays were few and far between. He would have money from his corn long before this account was anywhere near depleted. But just keeping even or a little ahead wasn't exactly riches.

Lou carefully folded the two bills and thrust them into his pocket. Damn, but a man gained two feet in stature when he had money in his pocket.

Mills didn't seem too busy, and Lou welcomed the chance to talk to him. He didn't know how long Nalley would be in Parnell's office, but it shouldn't be much longer.

"It looks like a good year, doesn't it, Lou?" Mills asked.

Mills seemed eager to talk. Lou supposed Mills didn't often have a sympathetic ear. He thought again of how awful it would be to have to work for a man like Welles Parnell.

"It sure does." Lou's voice was filled with enthusiasm. "I can't remember when everything looked so good at this time of the year."

Mills sighed. "I hope so. For everybody. Last year was a strained one for most people."

Lou couldn't resist saying, "If it isn't a good year Welles will have some more farms on his hands. I hear he's foreclosed on three more farms. What's he trying to do? Grab up all the land in the county?"

Mills's face froze in disapproving lines. "Mr. Parnell believes in the future of land in this county. You make it sound as though Mr. Parnell steals those farms."

"Not illegally," Lou stated. "But I never heard of him giving anybody an extra margin of time."

Mills was stiff with resentment, and his head bent to his work. He couldn't have said it louder. Mills wanted no more conversation with Lou.

Lou swore at himself. He should have known how old Charley

would react to somebody badmouthing his boss. Lou could say one thing; Mills was loyal to Parnell.

Lou looked at the office door. It was still closed. Damn it, what was taking Nalley so long? Mills was absorbed in real or imaginary work, and he wouldn't look at Lou.

Lou felt like a fool standing here and being ignored. He hadn't said anything for which he felt an apology was due, and he certainly had no intention of trying to soothe Mills's ruffled feelings. He could wait outside of the bank just as well as in here.

"Be seeing you, Charley," he said and sauntered toward the door.

"Sure," Mills mumbled, but he still wouldn't look up.

Lou looked back at the office door just before he stepped outside. He hoped Nalley wasn't running into any trouble.

Lou stepped out onto the walk, still looking at the office door. He bumped squarely into someone and grunted at the impact.

"I'm sorry," he said in quick apology. "I didn't mean—" He looked at Phil Herrick, and his jaw hardened. He wasn't apologizing to Herrick for anything.

"Why don't you watch where you're going, you hick?" Herrick said savagely.

"Who in the hell do you think you are to call me that?" Lou exploded. He was so furious he didn't see the glint in Herrick's eyes.

"Maybe this will help you remember who I am," Herrick said and threw a punch.

Herrick was fast with his fists. Lou saw the blow coming but not in time to avoid the full impact against his jaw. Its force exploded in his head, dropping a thick black curtain over his eyes. The blackness was shot through by startling slashes of red. Lou felt the bones in his legs melting, and they would no longer support him. He went down, landing hard on his shoulder blades. He wasn't out, but everything was fuzzy, and he couldn't think too well. One thought pounded in his mind with clarion strokes. Doyle had told him a long time ago, if you're going to have trouble with a man, don't try to jawbone your way out of it. Hit him first, then argue over it later. Lou had made the cardinal mistake of forgetting that piece of advice.

"Come on, hick," a mocking voice sounded from far away. "Or are you just going to quit like I expected?"

Lou raised his head. Things were beginning to form up a little, for those wavering lines were solidifying into a single image. Instead of seeing three Herrick faces, there was now only one.

"Don't go away," Lou said thickly.

What Herrick said didn't grate Lou nearly as much as the following laughter. That scraped skin off of Lou's soul.

He rolled over and tried to lift himself by his arms. They kept buckling on him, dumping him into the dust each time he put a little weight on them. His breathing sobbed in his throat as he cursed those treacherous arms.

"What the hell's going on here?" a familiar voice roared from the bank's doorway.

Lou didn't have to turn his head to recognize that voice. Nalley was coming out of the bank.

Lou looked at him. Nalley and Parnell were in the doorway. Evidently, Parnell had walked to the door with Nalley.

"Stay out of this, Sam," Lou begged. "It's my business."

Herrick's startled glance swept over Nalley and Parnell. He muttered something, then scurried down the street.

Nalley wanted to charge after him, but Lou managed to stop him.

"Let it go, Sam," he said thickly. Lou almost raised himself that time. One more effort, and he could make it. The physical hurt didn't cause him nearly the agony as the gloating look on Parnell's face.

Nalley rushed out to Lou and bent over him. He hauled Lou to his feet, and Lou sagged against him as his legs threatened to buckle again. But his head was perfectly clear; he could think. His jaw hurt, and he raised a hand to it. There was a definite knot there, and Lou was certain the swelling would grow larger.

"He nailed me a good one, Sam," Lou said and tried to grin. The gloating remained on Parnell's face, and Lou yelled at him. "What the hell are you standing there for?" he said furiously.

Parnell's face burned a bright red, but he turned and went back into the bank.

"I didn't want him seeing that," Lou complained.

"I'd think you'd rather it hadn't happened at all," Nalley said. He looked concerned. "What was that about?"

"It was my fault, Sam. I ran into him." This time Lou was to blame. But all the build-up that preceded this wasn't his fault.

Nalley rumbled deep in his throat. "By God, I wish I'd been out here. I want just one crack at that son of a bitch." He paused. "Lou, was this over a woman?"

Lou felt the heat crawl up from his collar into his face. "What makes you say a damnfool thing like that?" he asked angrily.

Nalley gestured helplessly. "Lou, it's all over town that Herrick is sweet on Celia. Everytime she goes outside of Storhmier's Herrick is with her. This looked like woman trouble to me."

"Damn it, Sam," Lou said hotly. "Will you drop it?"

Nalley had never seen Lou so angry. He shrugged and said, "If that's the way you want it. But I think you ought to tell Briner about this. He'd do something about it."

Sure, Briner would do something about this, if Lou preferred charges, but Lou couldn't stand to think of the publicity such a charge would bring. And even more, this would incur Briner's further displeasure. Briner would want to know what Herrick and Lou were brawling about before Welles's bank. Lou didn't have an answer that would satisfy Briner.

Lou stubbornly shook his head. "It's something I've got to take care of myself, Sam."

Nalley was familiar with Lou's stubborn streak. "All right, Lou," he said and sighed. "I'm just damned sorry it happened."

Lou tried to laugh and failed. "That's two of us, Sam. Are you all finished with Parnell?"

Nalley nodded.

"I didn't get the groceries I came in for," Lou said. "Let me stop at Arnold's, and I'll be right with you."

"Go ahead," Nalley replied. "I'll bring the buggy over."

Lou nodded and walked the block to Arnold's store. He was going to remember that incident with Herrick for some time. Maybe Parnell seeing him down in the street hurt as much as Herrick's blow.

Lou walked inside the store and greeted the man behind the counter. "Hello, Hap."

If Arnold was aware of Lou's encounter with Herrick, or the swelling jaw, he didn't comment.

"How are things going, Lou?" Arnold asked cheerfully.

Happy Arnold must be at least seventy, but his blue eyes were as bright as ever, and he was as spry as a cricket. Arnold had a boundless enthusiasm for everything he did. Lou recognized it was a good way to live. But how in the hell did one acquire that outlook? Arnold must have been born with that trait.

"Need a few things, Hap," Lou said. He pulled a short list from his shirt pocket and scanned it. "I need flour and sugar and salt. Better give me a slab of bacon. Yes, give me a jug of molasses and a box of ginger snaps." Those would be his sole catering to a sweet tooth.

Arnold never ceased chattering as he hopped about filling Lou's order. "Got a price on canned beans," Arnold suggested.

Lou nodded. "Better give me a dozen cans. Don't want to be running into town every other day."

Arnold kept making suggestions. Lou refused most of them. Now and then, he nodded agreement. "I guess that about does it, Hap. Total it up."

That was quite a pile of groceries on the counter. Lou bought more than he intended when he came in here. It took a big bite out of a ten-dollar bill. Oh well, he wouldn't have to buy groceries for another month or so.

Nalley came in just as Arnold finished bagging Lou's groceries. He picked up one of the sacks and grunted. "Looks like you were trying to buy out the store."

Lou chuckled. "Not quite." He picked up the other bag and said, "See you again, Hap."

Nalley untied the mare while Lou put the sacks in the buggy. They climbed up to the seat and Nalley clucked to the mare. They were almost out of town before Nalley spoke. "Groceries are damned expensive," he grumbled. "Scares the hell out of a man just to think about them."

Lou knew Nalley was trying to make conversation to ease Lou through an awkward moment. It was up to Lou whether or not he wanted to speak further about Herrick knocking him down.

Lou rubbed his chin and said, "Sore."

"I imagine," Nalley said matter-of-factly. He waited for a long moment, then no longer able to hold his words, burst out, "I can't imagine you just taking that without doing something about it."

Lou's voice hardened. "That'll come later, Sam." He debated upon telling Nalley that Celia was the basis of all this mess. But it would make him feel so damned foolish and awkward. Maybe she hadn't asked Herrick to do anything about Lou's corn, and she hadn't asked Herrick to knock him down. But her interest in Herrick was behind both of those things. Lou knew one thing for sure. Celia had to make up her mind whether she was interested in Herrick or Lou Manard. He rubbed his jaw again. Right now, he didn't care which way she decided. He thought in sudden anguish. You can't even lie to yourself. You do care.

CHAPTER ELEVEN

Nalley pulled the buggy up before Lou's house and helped him carry the groceries inside. Lou was afraid Nalley wanted to leave, and he needed somebody to talk to.

"Sam, are you in a big hurry?"

Nalley caught the appeal in Lou's question. "No hurry at all, Lou. The trip gave me a thirst. I'm dry enough to even try some of your coffee."

Lou smiled at the gentle raillery. Nalley was doing everything he could to lift Lou's spirits. "I bought a box of ginger snaps, Sam. How about some of them?"

Nalley grinned. "Hell, yes. That would disguise the taste of your coffee."

"Someday, I'm going to surprise you, Sam, and make you a decent cup of coffee."

Nalley hooted at him. "I'll believe that when I see it."

Lou pulled several sticks out of the wood box and built a fire in the stove. This stove always drew well, and it wasn't long before a leaping fire was going.

Lou stepped outside and dumped the old coffee grounds onto the ground. "That's in your honor," he said solemnly as he came back inside. "Those weren't old grounds. Only been using them the last couple of weeks."

Nalley chuckled, and his eyes sparkled. He felt good and showed it.

The coffee began to boil, and its aroma permeated the room. "It smells good," Lou announced. "I don't care what you say."

"Even smells good to me," Nalley agreed.

Lou poured two cups full, and Nalley tasted his. Mock surprise crossed his face. "Say, this is good coffee. You must have bought a new brand."

Lou grinned wanly. He wished he felt as good as Nalley sounded.

"How about going out to the swing, Sam?"

"Always liked that swing," Nalley said. "This time, I can enjoy it. Sarah's not around yelling at me for loafing."

"You lead a tough life," Lou said sardonically. He carried his cup and the ginger snaps to the swing.

They sat side by side, Lou moving his foot just enough to keep the swing moving gently. The swing's chains creaked rhythmically, and the insects droned on in the two big maple trees.

"Always liked those trees," Nalley commented. "Many a time I thought of digging them up and replanting them before my house. Only thing that stopped me was I felt it might make you sore."

That pulled a weak laugh out of Lou. "That's probably the only thing I'd shoot you for."

"I was afraid you'd feel like that," Nalley said. He bit into another snap. "Not bad at all. Arnold must have gotten in a fresh supply."

Lou watched a bunch of his hens come around the corner of the house. They kept up that low clucking, and Lou wondered if they were communicating with each other. He never knew of anybody who could say with authority. The rooster was usually behind the hens. Ah, there he came, strutting after the hens.

He made a sudden dash toward an unsuspecting hen, caught her by surprise, and thoroughly mauled her while he worked his will. He let her up, and she squawked indignantly while she shook her ruffled feathers back into place. The rooster threw back its head and crowed, telling the world what a big man he was.

"One thing I can say for a rooster," Lou burst out. "He doesn't have any trouble with his womenfolk."

Nalley stared quizzically at Lou. "You having trouble with your womenfolk, Lou?"

Lou grinned painfully. "Sounds like I'm bragging, doesn't it, Sam? I thought I knew where I was going. Now, I'm lost."

It was out, and Lou had to go ahead and talk about it. Saying this to Maude's father was going to be difficult, but Lou had to have somebody to talk to.

"Sam, I proposed to Celia." Was that a catch in Nalley's breathing? Lou couldn't be sure.

Nalley stared out into the yard for a long moment. "She turn you down?" he asked quietly.

Lou shook his head. "She hasn't made up her mind, Sam. I guess we had our first quarrel."

"Doesn't amount to anything," Nalley said. "When you get married, you'll learn how to avoid quarrels or to live with them."

"That's not exactly it, Sam," Lou said. He watched a line of ants cross his porch. That was supposed to signify fair weather. When ants scattered, it was supposed to mean stormy weather.

"I guess I did some bragging to Celia about my prospects," Lou went on. "She said something about them to Herrick. He tore down that fence."

Nalley sucked in his breath. "Ah," he said in fuller understanding. "Herrick hit you because of Celia."

"I guess he did," Lou admitted.

"What are you going to do about it?" Nalley asked bluntly. He impatiently shook his head at Lou's long silence. "You haven't made up your mind yet, have you?"

"I told you I asked her to marry me," Lou cried.

"Not enough," Nalley said decisively. "The question is, do you want to marry her?"

"Yes." The word was said without too long a hesitation.

"You don't sound too positive to me," Nalley stated. "Let me tell you something, boy. If you've got any doubts at all, run like hell. It could be a warning."

"But I asked her to marry me," Lou cried.

"Oh Jesus," Nalley moaned. "An honorable man. You've got doubts, or you wouldn't be talking to me about this. You're asking me what to do. I can't tell you that. That's your decision. I think I know what's trapped you. A pretty female face. It's the biggest trap of all." He tapped his forefinger on Lou's thigh. "I will tell you this. Do a lot of thinking before you make a mistake that would scar you for life."

He tried to chuckle at Lou's woebegone face. "Not much consolation, is it? You're asking something that's impossible for another man to deliver. You want a map with your road clearly marked out. Nobody can do that."

"I guess you're right," Lou muttered. "How about some more coffee?"

Nalley wanted to say something else; it was written all over his face. Instead, he sighed again and shook his head. "Not much help, am I?"

"No," Lou admitted honestly. "But thanks for letting me talk to you." He picked up the coffee cups and headed for the door. He felt better after talking to Nalley. He saw no clear-cut solutions to his worry, but there was a relief in just talking. Maybe his heart and head were warring over Celia. He'd just have to go along and see which won.

Lou paused before he entered the house. What was that faint, far-away sound? He frowned, trying to identify it. It sounded like a swarm of bees when they transferred to a new bee tree. But this sound had far greater volume.

"What are you listening to?" Nalley asked. "I don't hear anything."

The sound steadily grew in volume. "Can't you hear it now, Sam?"

"I do now. Is that faraway thunder?"

Lou shook his head. Distant thunder had a rumbling roll. He had looked up at the sky when he and Nalley returned from town. There hadn't been a cloud in the sky, not even on the horizon.

Lou came back to the swing and set the cups on it. "I don't think so, Sam. But we'd better find out what it is."

He walked around the house, Nalley at his heels.

"My God," Lou said in awe. "Look at that!"

The northwestern sky was darkened as though a vast cloud of thick, dark smoke drifted lazily toward them. The darkening of the sky stretched sideways as far as Lou could see and reached back to the horizon. The sound had grown in volume until Lou had to raise his voice to make Nalley hear him.

"God," he yelped. "That's grasshoppers. Millions of them."

Nalley stared at the sky, his mouth agape.

The cloud drifted over them, and the humming of the insects' wings filled a man's head until he could think of nothing else. The first wave of insects started sailing to the ground.

"Grasshoppers," Nalley said in shock. "My grandpa told me of grasshopper plagues. What he saw couldn't be as bad as this."

Lou went a little crazy. He looked as though he was dancing in place, each boot heel slamming hard against the ground. He killed dozens of grasshoppers with every stamp, and he didn't have to move from one spot. For every grasshopper he killed, a multitude took its place. A thousand stamping men couldn't have made an appreciable dent in the insects' numbers. In the space of a few breaths the ground was covered with grasshoppers. Still they kept coming, crawling over those already on the ground. The two maple trees and every plant were covered, until their outlines were a solid mass of crawling insects. They stung a man's face as they sailed into his flesh. Lou stamped until he was breathless.

Nalley had been doing the same thing, and now he stopped. "This won't do any good," he said in a tired, defeated voice.

The fact that Nalley was right drove Lou wild. He couldn't just stand here and see everything he worked for vanish. The trees were stripped of their leaves in a few minutes' time. Lou swore he could hear the click of the insects' rapacious jaws.

Nalley looked sick. "What are we going to do, Lou?"

The same sickness was in Lou's eyes. He thought of a dozen courses of action, and every one seemed futile. How could a man fight a hungry horde like this?

"I don't know." Lou's words were an admission he was beaten.

The chickens were in paradise. They darted about the yard, their beaks stabbing at the grasshoppers. They didn't have to expend much energy. They could stand in one place and gorge themselves. Some of them already showed the effects of their unlimited feeding. Their craws were swollen, showing like small balloons in their necks. In a few minutes' time, they were no longer able to dart about. When they moved, it was with a sluggish waddle.

Lou wanted to rave and swear, but he didn't know at whom to direct the invective. He turned his head toward Nalley. "Sam, it won't do any good to stand here, watching this. Wait until I get Dandy saddled. We'll ride over to your place."

"You think it will be any better there?" Nalley asked bitterly.

Lou didn't. He would bet the entire country had been hit with this plague. "No," he answered. "But maybe having us there will be some solace to the women."

Nalley nodded in dumb agreement. Lou turned toward the barn. He heard the familiar crunch with every step. The damned pests were even in the barn. They wouldn't find much to eat in here.

The insects crawled over the animals. The horses' ears twitched back and forth, and ripple after ripple ran down their hides, trying to dislodge the crawling annoyances. Much more of this would set them wild.

Dandy was hard to handle, and Lou had to calm him down before he could saddle him. "Easy, boy, easy," he soothed the stallion, as he swept the grasshoppers from his hide. He couldn't resist stepping on them, and he ground his heel against the hard-packed earth.

He mounted Dandy and rode around the house. From this short distance, Lou could see a corner of his cornfield. He resolutely kept his eyes turned from the field, knowing what he would see. Only a few moments before, even considering his personal problems, he had felt relatively good. Now he felt as thoroughly beaten as though a dozen men had worked him over with clubs.

Nalley was already seated in the buggy, and Lou paused beside it long enough to ask, "Ready to go, Sam?"

Nalley answered Lou's question with one of his own. "Why, Lou? For God's sake, why?"

Lou irritably shook his head. Nobody could answer that. "I'll follow you, Sam," he said shortly.

A small creek ran between Lou and Nalley's places, and Nalley's buggy stopped at the beginning of the low water ford. Lou pulled up beside the vehicle.

"Did you ever see anything like this?" Nalley asked in an awe-stricken voice.

Lou's throat was so tight that it was difficult to force words to his tongue. He didn't think Nalley really expected an answer. Lou hoped he would never again see anything like this. Up and down the stream as far as they could see, the water's surface was covered with dead and dying grasshoppers. Their packed bodies gave the creek a greenish, scumlike appearance. Lou had seen a creek look like this before, but that had been in the dog days of late August when the moss was so thick it covered the water.

Feeding fish leaped out of the water, then fell back, leaving a momentarily cleared area. Then the area closed in, leaving a solid-looking greenish mass. Lou thought of his chickens. The fish were in the same paradise.

"Something is getting some good out of this." Lou made a feeble attempt at humor.

"Will the fish taste like grasshoppers after they get filled up on them?" Nalley asked absently.

Nalley could ask the damnedest questions. "How would I know something like that?" Lou returned sharply.

He saw then that was Nalley's attempt at weak humor, for a ghastly grin distorted Nalley's face. "I was just wondering, Lou," he explained. "I was just thinking that fish and chickens would be about all we have left to eat after the grasshoppers get through."

Lou forced a weak laugh in return. Nalley might have something at that. Dandy was dancing in place, and when Lou looked down at the stallion's forelegs, he saw the cause. Insects were crawling up Dandy's legs. Lou couldn't hold him much longer in this spot. For a moment, the wildness threatened to engulf him. Right now, he couldn't say there was any spot in the whole land that wasn't infested.

Nalley stared at the creek as though mesmerized, and Lou said, "We better get moving along, Sam."

Nalley jerked as though he came out of a deep reverie. "You're right," he muttered and lifted the reins.

The mare crossed the low-water bridge, splashing water to both sides. For a brief moment, Lou caught sight of the creek's clear water, then the slime closed in again.

"Let's go, Dandy," Lou said harshly. Dandy didn't like it any better than Lou did.

He splashed across the creek, following Nalley's buggy. Lou imagined he could hear the crunch of insect bodies, for the road was covered with the grasshoppers. He wanted to give way to an insane desire to laugh, afraid that if he didn't, he would burst into tears.

Maude and Sarah were on the front porch when Lou and Nalley arrived. Sarah held the screen door open while Maude swept frantically at the insects on the floor. She worked as though possessed as she whisked grasshoppers out of the door. She went back for another swath and swept out as many grasshoppers as before. Lou couldn't see where she was making much progress.

Maude dropped her broom as she saw Lou dismount and ran toward him. He absently noticed the reddish glint in the luxurious crown of her black hair. Her face was contorted, and she tried to fight off her emotions, but she was very close to the breaking point.

"Easy, Maude," Lou said, trying to console her.

She drew a deep breath, then was able to smile. "Isn't it awful?"

"Pretty bad." Lou was afraid she was going to cry, and he patted her on the arm.

She shook her head angrily, and Lou didn't know whether it was protest against her weakness or his touch.

Her words solved that for him. "Oh, Lou," she wailed. "I hate the damned, crawling things so. I step on them everywhere I walk." A shudder ran through her. "When I look down—" She turned pale and didn't finish the sentence.

"Pretty messy, isn't it?" Lou said matter-of-factly. "It's just as bad at my place." He wanted to assure her she wasn't alone.

"Lou, what are we going to do?" Maude cried. "The house is filled with them."

Lou hadn't been able to answer Nalley's questions either, and here

Maude hit him with another one. He looked up at the sky, and it was clear. He doubted any more grasshoppers were coming.

"I don't think it'll get any worse, Maude." Lou grimaced at the poor consolation of his words. They had more than they could handle right now.

"Lou, I'm so glad you're here," Maude said soberly.

Lou knew there was no personal nuance in what she said. She just needed companionship in this moment of stress. The earth was crawling or heaving. If a person had to face this alone, it could easily drive one crazy.

Maude took a step and shuddered. Her step produced the same crunching sound from underfoot.

Nalley checked with Lou before he followed Maude. "Lou, want to leave Dandy in the barn?"

Lou started to say he wouldn't be here that long, then held the words. He had no idea of how long he would be here, but he couldn't leave his friends at a time like this.

Nalley's barn was probably like his own, the inside of it crawling with the insects, but it might give Dandy a small protection against those itchy, scratchy feet.

"Might be an idea, Sam," he said.

Lou tied Dandy to a manger and stripped the saddle and blanket from him. He felt helpless, for he didn't know what to do with the saddle.

"Sam, do you suppose they'll chew on a saddle?"

"Lord, Lou, I don't know. They're all over my tool handles. Do you suppose the damned things will eat them too?"

Lou didn't know much about grasshoppers, but he seriously considered Nalley's question. "No telling what they'll eat. It might be the taste of sweat they're after. You got a tarpaulin?"

At Nalley's bewildered nod, Lou went on, "Maybe a tarpaulin will stop them." He laid down his saddle and covered it with the tarp, then helped Nalley gather up his tools and place them beside the saddle. Together, they covered the saddle and tools.

"A hell of a note," Nalley said bitterly. "When a man has to go to this limit to protect his tools."

Lou could fully agree with him, but there was no use beating a question for which there was no answer. At least, they had done everything they could.

Sarah Nalley met them at the edge of the porch. "Lou," she said, the relief at his presence showing in her voice. Sarah hadn't yet given away to tears, but there was a suspicious moisture in her eyes. Her nerves had to be raw.

Lou opened the door for her.

"Lou," Maude wailed, waiting just inside the door. "There's just as many as there were before I started sweeping."

She, too, was close to tears. Lou took command. Both these women had fought the crawling insects for too long.

He propped the door open with a chair. Sam had followed him inside and stood there, looking helpless.

"Sam, go around the room and knock the damned things from the walls," Lou ordered. "I'll sweep them out."

His strokes were vigorous and swift. He made one long last stroke at the door. The broom sent grasshoppers out of the door in one mighty sweep. Some of the insects flew, others rolled over and over. He was making progress. There were fewer insects in the room.

He turned a startled face toward Maude as she screamed.

"I'm sorry, Lou," she apologized. "One of them landed in my hair."

"Sure," he said flatly. He sympathized with her, but he couldn't show it. Sympathy might destroy the remnants of her self-control.

Lou finally got the last of the pests out of the house and closed the door. That would make the house hotter, but he couldn't help that. Of course, a few of the insects would creep back in, but the first onslaught had been turned back.

"If they just don't start chewing their way through the walls," he said with grim humor.

That brought a wan smile to Maude's lips. "Maybe I can laugh about it later, Lou. Right now, it isn't very amusing."

The sun's slanting rays reached across the room. Lou turned toward Nalley.

"Sam, we haven't got much time before darkness sets in. Let's split up and get to as many men as we can reach. Have everybody here in the morning."

Some of the despondency lifted from Nalley's face. "You've got an idea?"

Lou dashed Nalley's hopes by shaking his head. "Not in the least, Sam. But maybe if we can get several heads together, somebody will come up with something."

"You'll be back for supper, Lou?" Sarah asked.

Lou thought there was hesitation behind the offer. He couldn't look at Maude.

"Maybe another time," he said evenly.

He and Nalley walked outside, Nalley to his wagon, and Lou to saddle Dandy. Looking around made Lou sick to his stomach. The insects were everywhere, busily devouring anything green. Poor Maude, Lou thought. She'll grieve over her flowers. He glanced at the flower beds. The flowers couldn't be seen because of the grasshoppers. Give them another few minutes, and only the stalks would be left.

"You go east, Sam," Lou said. "Tell everyone to be here early in the morning. Somebody has to think of a way to fight this." He guessed he belonged in the same class as his chickens. He had never felt so empty-headed in his life.

He lifted his hand to Nalley, turned Dandy and kicked him into motion. Each hoof stirred up small clouds of insects. Their wings whirred as they sailed off, only to settle in another place.

Lou was drained of all oaths. He knew how much damage the grasshoppers could do to young corn. They could easily kill the tender plants overnight.

CHAPTER TWELVE

Eight men were gathered at Nalley's shortly after the sun rose. Each man reported the same infestation of the grasshoppers.

"When they first landed, I went crazy," Silas Eldridge said. He was a big, strapping man, able to cope with the ordinary events of a day, but this onslaught had whipped him. "I ran up and down the corn rows, trying to knock them off and stamp on them. I couldn't get beyond the fourth stalk before the first was covered again with the damned things."

Lou nodded in somber agreement. "It's happening to all of us. That's why I wanted this meeting. I hoped somebody would come up with a suggestion of how to fight them."

He looked at the faces about him. There was nothing encouraging in those faces. Everybody seemed as baffled as he was about a course of action.

"The goddamned things are eating their heads off," Mellinger exploded. "I lay there all night, thinking I could hear them chewing away." He scowled at the others. "Don't try to eat any eggs. I tried some for breakfast. I took a couple of bites and quit. They weren't fit to eat. They tasted like grasshoppers."

"How do you know?" Nabor jeered. "Did you ever taste a grasshopper before?"

The question brought out a couple of pained chuckles.

"All right," Mellinger bristled. He wasn't in a mood to join in any kind of humor. "It wasn't my imagination. Those eggs tasted funny."

"The wife won't let me get in the house until I clean my shoes," Tilden said moodily. "She won't have me tracking greasy smears into her house." He contemplated his big, rawboned knuckles. "How's a man going to do his chores without stepping on the blasted things?" He glanced around, his jaw jutting out. He would just like to hear someone come up with a solution to that problem.

Every one of these men was going on raw nerves. Lou thought they would be quarreling with each other in a moment.

"Stop it," Lou said sharply. "All of us are going through the same thing. We've got enough troubles without jawboning at each other. We can't just sit on our asses and not try to do something. Anybody got an idea? I don't care how crazy it sounds."

"If there was only some way we could poison them," Nabor ventured. He sighed and shook his head.

"That's a real fine idea," Mellinger said sourly. "How are you going to get it to them? Carry it around and force it down their throats?"

Nabor flared at the criticism. "I don't hear you suggesting anything better."

"Oh, for God's sake," Lou said wearily. "He's not jumping on you, Nabor. Say we had the poison, how would we use it?"

Nabor sighed. "Forget it. I knew it was a crazy idea the moment I said it."

Eldridge spoke up. "I even thought of trying to pick them off my corn and drop them into a gunny bag. Don't laugh. I found out in a hurry it'd take a million gunny bags. Even that many wouldn't make much of a dent."

Nabor gnawed off a chew of tobacco and tucked it into his cheek. His jaws worked, then he spit an amber stream over Nalley's porch railing.

"That looks just like the juice a grasshopper spits," Mellinger said absently.

Nabor took the remark as a personal insult. It enraged him so much he almost swallowed his cud.

Before Nabor could speak, Lou roared, "Hold it." These men had lived on friendly terms for years. A few more unwise words could destroy a relationship of long standing.

An idea was forming in Lou's mind, but it was rough. "Eldridge, you said something about filling a gunny bag with hoppers, but that would be too slow. If we could gather them up faster—"

Mellinger's mood hadn't improved, and he interrupted Lou. "Are you suggesting cutting up several gunny bags and making one big one out of them?" he scoffed.

"Something like that," Lou said calmly. The hazy outline of his idea began to take shape. "Maybe we won't actually have to make that big gunny bag."

He had their attention now. "Why couldn't we tack a long piece of canvas to a frame and suspend it from a couple of horses? Sam, you've got a large piece of canvas in the barn. We covered up my saddle and your tools with it yesterday. Two men could drive those horses, keeping them abreast of each other. We could drive down several rows and bag a hell of a lot of hoppers."

"That would break down corn," Nabor said doubtfully.

Lou looked at Nabor a moment, keeping firm control on his temper. All of them had the right to pick an idea to pieces. That was what this meeting was for; to twist and turn an idea around until something came out of it that could be formulated into a solid course of action. "If it doesn't work, are we any worse off than we are now?" Lou asked evenly.

"God, no," Eldridge exploded.

"Sam, have you got some fairly light, long boards we can tack the canvas on?" Lou saw protests forming on several faces. "We're all here," he said. "We might as well see if it works on Sam's corn."

A pathetic eagerness appeared in Nalley's eyes, and he tried to disguise it. "I wouldn't want to be first—"

"We're wasting time," Lou pointed out. He wasn't sure how that long screen could be suspended between two horses, and he poked and probed at the thought. Maybe they would need a rider on each horse to hold the frame. He would still need a driver for each horse, for the riders would need all their strength and attention to hold up the canvas.

"Well?" he asked.

"I guess we might as well try it," Tilden muttered.

All of them tramped down to the barn. Nalley went in and came out with the canvas. "I'm afraid it's got some rips in it."

Lou grinned. "Then a few of the bugs will slip through."

"I've got some boards on the other side of the barn," Nalley said. "Maybe we can find what we want."

Lou went through the pile of boards, picking and discarding. The men watched him, and Lou could feel their doubt hitting him like a tangible wave. He didn't blame them. He wasn't sure what he was doing, and even if he managed to build something out of these boards, he wasn't sure the contraption would work.

Nalley helped him straighten out the canvas. Lou paced it off. By rough measurement the canvas was twelve feet long and six feet wide. He wanted to build a frame that would take out the limpness of the canvas.

To get the proper length, Lou nailed two boards together. He picked up the long length and hefted its weight. It wouldn't be anything to handle for a man with his feet on the ground, but Lou could appreciate the tremendous strain on a man's arms when he was astride a horse. This was only one of the long sides of the frame Lou had in mind. Add the weight of the canvas to the finished frame— Lou shut off the thought, or he would be visualizing a total weight they couldn't even get off the ground.

Lou knew a flash of resentment at the watching faces. All of them looked so hopeful. Damn it, he was no miracle worker. He couldn't guarantee them a thing. Then, the resentment went away. They weren't against him, they just wanted so badly to see this thing work.

Lou found two five-foot boards, wanting to leave a belly in the depth of the canvas.

Nalley helped him lay out the canvas on the finished frame. "I'm going to have to put a lot of nail holes in your canvas, Sam," Lou said.

"Do whatever you have to," Nalley agreed. "I'm only praying it will work."

All of us are, Lou thought as he started hammering in the nails.

Nalley found another hammer and started on the other end. When they finished, they had a belly in the canvas at the bottom side of the frame. Lou was satisfied with the pocket it formed. If this thing worked at all, it should scoop up a lot of grasshoppers.

Lou lifted one end while Eldridge lifted the other. The frame was awkward and flimsy, but held horizontally, it should be able to hold the weight of many hoppers.

"What do you think, Silas?" Lou asked.

"Not too bad," Eldridge decided. "But will it hold the weight of the grasshoppers?"

"I don't know," Lou confessed. He didn't know a lot of things about this canvas-covered frame. If it didn't work, he could just imagine how disappointed all of them would be.

Lou climbed onto Molly. Thank God, he hadn't brought Dandy this morning. He almost laughed at the thought of how Dandy would react to something like this. He would bolt before he took a half-dozen strides, scattering pieces of frame and canvas all over the county. Molly was a placid horse; she would do whatever Lou asked of her.

Eldridge mounted Nalley's mare. The horses showed some uneasiness when the rack was handed up to the two riders. Lou talked to Molly, quieting her down, and he heard Eldridge soothing Nalley's mare.

The mares settled down, and Lou appointed Nabor and Nalley to drive the two horses with long reins attached to the bits.

"Keep them straight," he said. "Or you'll pull one of us off."

Nalley nodded grimly, and Nabor was tight-lipped. Both of them knew only too well what could happen.

"The rest of you start digging a pit," Lou said.

"By God, if that don't sound like useless work to me," Mellinger yelled. "What good is that going—"

Lou cut him short. "What do you think we're going to do with the grasshoppers we collect?" Lou asked impatiently. "Can you think of a better way of getting ride of them than burying them?"

"I guess you got something," Mellinger grumbled. "Nalley, you got any shovels?"

"In the barn," Nalley answered shortly. Like the others, he was tight-lipped. He was getting sick of Mellinger's bellyaching.

Mellinger came back from the barn with an assorted armload of shovels. He was in a foul mood, and his face showed it. "I'll be god-damned, if they haven't started chewing on the handles. Look at this!"

Men gathered around Mellinger to inspect the damage. "Give them a few more hours, and they'd chew clear through those handles," Riley said in awe.

Lou and Nalley exchanged significant glances. They had tried yesterday evening to protect against this very thing, but now the protecting canvas was being used for another purpose.

"Better get started on that digging," Lou suggested. He stared at Mellinger until Mellinger looked away. Damn him, Lou thought. Lou didn't want to order anybody around. All he wanted to do was to find out if this idea was worth a damn.

Even before the cornfield was reached, Lou thought with a burst of hope, it's going to work. Each step the horses took stirred up a new cloud of insects, and the belly in the canvas pocketed them. Before the grasshoppers could crawl out or fly away, new arrivals smothered them by sheer weight.

"By God, I think it's working," Nalley shouted.

Lou didn't answer. All his attention was on the frame he and Eldridge were holding. Both men had to lean far out with both hands holding the frame close to the ground. The weight of the collected insects was mounting appreciably. Already, Lou felt the pull on his arms.

Nabor and Nalley hesitated before they sent the horses into the field.

Lou knew the cause for their hesitation. Both men hated the thought of breaking down the corn.

"Keep moving," Lou yelled. "We're losing some."

He glanced at the corn before Molly started moving again. Good Lord! Already the damage to the field could be plainly seen. Most of the leaves hung in tatters, and on others only the heavy veins of the leaf remained.

The moving horses kept a steady cloud of insects rising. They hit against the canvas and dropped into the belly of the improvised screen.

The pull on Lou's arms steadily increased. Eldridge felt it too, for he called, "My arms are about ready to drop off."

Lou nodded. "We've got enough this run." He was appalled by the small area they had covered. Not over thirty feet, he judged.

"Turn the horses slow and easy," he called back. If Nalley and Nabor didn't act in unison, they could easily jerk the frame out of the riders' hands.

Nalley and Nabor kept the mares together as they made a careful turn. Lou watched the squirming mass of life in the canvas pocket. They were losing hoppers with every step, but that couldn't be helped.

The pit wasn't as deep or as long as Lou would have liked. He looked at the sweating faces of the diggers and held his tongue. The men had dug as fast and hard as they could.

Riley looked at the grasshoppers, and his mouth hung open. "Jesus! You must've collected a million of them."

Lou grinned wearily. "Maybe not that many. Give us some help with this frame."

Willing hands grasped the side boards and carried the frame to the shallow pit. They dumped out the squirming mass.

Lou took a shovel from Riley's hands. "Start burying them."

Grasshoppers flew up out of the pit, and others crawled up the sides. Mellinger beat at the escaping insects with his shovel blade.

"Let them go," Lou said. "We've got the bulk in the pit."

Dirt from all angles flew into the pit. Lou took a breather when the pit was only half filled, but the insects were covered. An occasional grasshopper shook off its shroud and crawled up the side. It wasn't worth going after the few that escaped.

"Feel like another trip?" Lou asked Eldridge.

Eldridge rolled his shoulders to ease the ache in them. "I guess so." His enthusiasm wasn't ebbing; it was just his vitality that was fading.

The second trip produced just as many grasshoppers. This method was too slow to be successful. It took too long to dig the pits and too long to fill them. Lou hated to admit it even to himself, but there seemed to be as many grasshoppers in the area already covered, as there were on the first trip. They dumped the hoppers into the pit, and again it was a mad race to shovel enough dirt on them to prevent them climbing out.

"We've killed a lot of them," Riley said. There was no elation in his voice. The enormity of the task was beginning to overwhelm him, too.

Lou's mind picked at the problem. They were gathering many of the grasshoppers, but the digging of the pit, then the time spent in covering it, was wrecking them. They had to come up with something faster.

"Kerosene," he burst out. Lou grinned at the startled faces turned toward him. "I haven't lost my mind. I was just wondering if kerosene would kill them. If it doesn't we could douse them thoroughly, then set the kerosene afire."

"It'd take a hell of a lot of kerosene," Mellinger complained.

"There's a hell of a lot of grasshoppers, too," Lou said savagely. "Sam, do you have any kerosene?"

"I just broached a new drum, Lou. It may not do any good, but I'd get pleasure from seeing the damn things burn."

Three men went with Nalley to help carry the drum back. Lou heard the sloshing of the liquid as the drum was set down.

"Ready to go back?" Lou asked.

Eldridge shook his head. "I'll dig this time."

Tilden climbed on Nalley's mare. "Let's go," he said.

The riders and drivers made another sweep into the field and returned with another load of insects and dumped them into a freshly dug pit. Cans of kerosene were dipped out of the drum and splashed on the crawling insects. Kerosene did kill the grasshoppers. Some of them kicked and bucked convulsively. The crawling insects, trying to get up the banks, dropped weakly back. Kerosene would work all right. Lou only wished they had enough of the stuff to fill a small pond.

"Light it," he said.

Nalley struck a match and tossed it into the pit. The kerosene was slow in catching, then the first small licking flame appeared. The flame swelled until a small inferno roared. The stench of the burning insects was sickening. Lou learned in a hurry not to stand windward of it.

The flame didn't last long, but it wasn't necessary. The heat generated was a killer in itself.

Nalley looked at the charred mass in the pit. "That did me a lot of good."

Lou laughed. "Then let's go back and get you some more pleasure."

They labored through the long day. Lou lost track of how many loads of insects they dumped and burned. He couldn't see where they were gaining much. They could go back over the same area and get almost as many grasshoppers as they had on previous trips.

Lou was ready to abandon the effort, but Nalley wouldn't have it. "I tell you it's doing some good," he said stubbornly.

Lou looked at the others to see how they felt. Every man was dog-tired. One by one they gave reluctant nods of defeat.

"I'm through," Mellinger said petulantly. "If I could see where we're doing any good, I'd be for it. But it's useless."

Nalley tried to persuade Mellinger. "How can you say that, Bill? Why, we must have killed millions."

Mellinger's jaw set obdurately. "And there's a million times that many still out there. While we're trying to save your field, what's happening to mine?"

Nalley blushed guiltily, and Lou spoke up in a hurry. "We all agreed on Sam's field," he said harshly. "Nobody's got you chained, if you want to leave."

Mellinger gave Lou a startled look, then turned and walked away, his shoulders stiff.

"Good riddance," Nabor said. "All he did was bellyache." He grinned sheepishly. "I guess he got on my nerves."

"Everybody's nerves are raw," Lou said. He made a vague gesture toward Nalley's cornfield. "What's happened out there is enough to make anybody swear at an angel."

Nabor chuckled, a rare sound for this day. "I'd swear to that. What about it? Do we keep on trying?"

Nalley wanted to; his eyes begged them to keep on.

"We're about out of kerosene, Sam," Lou said gently. "If we could find more kerosene in town, it would take time to go after it. It's all up to you."

Lou watched the collapse of Nalley's spirit. It left Nalley's face old and drawn.

"We didn't really do any good, did we?" Nalley's voice was lifeless.

Eldridge slapped him on the shoulder. "Not much, Sam. But nobody can say we didn't try. There's some things a man is up against—" he shook his head and didn't finish.

Nalley tried to regain his composure. "I can't tell you how grateful I am. I'll make it up to you one of these days."

The men made ribald remarks about his vow, then slowly drifted away.

"Good bunch of men," Nalley said, trying to put life into his voice.

Lou nodded. He could second that. He even forgave Mellinger for his behavior. The strain had been pretty rough.

His eyes widened in surprise. Nalley was laughing, a harsh, unpleasant burst of sound. Lou was afraid Nalley was cracking up. There certainly wasn't anything to laugh about.

"I heard your pa offer to pay for the damages his cows did to your field, Lou. You should have taken him up. It looks like that's the only money you could have made out of that field this year."

"Sure," Lou said gently. In a matter of a few hours Nalley had aged. He didn't look like the same man Lou had seen yesterday.

Lou turned toward the house, leading Molly, and Nalley led the other mare and fell into step with him.

"You'll come in and eat?" Nalley asked.

Lou shook his head. He was too tired to even think of eating. "I'll sit down for a minute, Sam. That's all. Right now, I don't think I could climb on Molly."

Maude came out of the house as the two walked up onto the porch. "Are you winning, Lou?" she asked. "I see just as many in the yard."

She realized the criticism in her words, for her mouth dropped open. "Oh, Lou," she wailed. "I didn't mean that the way it sounded."

"I know," Lou said soberly. "I don't know why, but I guess this was one battle we weren't supposed to win."

Maude stared at him a long agonized moment. Lou was sure she was going to break into tears. Then Maude whirled and ran into the house.

Lou and Nalley sat down in the two battered old rockers. Lou was too weary to even try to rock.

After a long silence Nalley said, "I guess this ruins me, Lou. The place is paid up for another year, but what am I going to do to bring in some money for food? There's nothing coming in from the crops this year. A man's got to have a little money to just live until next year."

Lou's heart ached for Nalley. Lou was one of the lucky ones. His place was free and clear. Disorganized thoughts ran through his mind, and a strong rebellion rose at the unfairness of it all. No one had tried any harder than Nalley, and his efforts didn't seem to amount to a damn. Lou thought of one thing after another, discarding each idea as impractical. But there had to be some way a man could survive until things grew better.

A new thought hit him all of a sudden, and he sat upright. "Maybe we've been planting the wrong crop, Sam. One year after another, it seems something always happens to corn. If it's not the drought, it's something like this. Maybe we ought to try something else."

"What would that be?" Nalley asked dully. "Corn is all I've ever planted."

"Wheat," Lou said decisively. "You heard me spout off the night I hit Parnell. If other parts of Kansas can do it, we can too."

Nalley shook his head, a sad, defeated gesture. "I don't see where that would do any good." A note of anger crept into his voice. "Would that stop what happened to us today?"

"Wheat's up far earlier than corn, and it's harvested sooner," Lou said reflectively. "Maybe we wouldn't miss another grasshopper plague, but we'd sure miss the summer's drought." He hoped Nalley could see what he was driving at. A drought was a lingering sickness, the grasshoppers wiped a man out in a hurry. He admitted, either way they faced ruin. But damn it, this was the first plague he had ever known, and he was sure Nalley could say the same. Lou's voice strengthened. If he couldn't convince Nalley, he had to convince himself.

"Sam, don't most of the droughts come in the summer? Wheat will be harvested by then. I'll take my chances of not having another grasshopper plague for a long time. It's worth a try, isn't it? At least, we ought to plant part of our acreage to wheat this fall."

Nalley's attempt at a laugh was a miserable failure. "Here you're talking about next year's crop. I'm just worrying about getting enough money for my family to last until then."

"We'll work out something, Sam." Lou didn't know what it would be, but something would turn up. If he didn't believe that, he might as well be dead. He wished he could promise Nalley something definite, but he was no miracle worker. Hadn't he learned that earlier?

Lou sat there, his mind picking at first one thing, then another. The immediate need was money; money for survival. He nodded as he thought of a possible solution. Maybe he had a way to get all of them eating money. He would have to find out if that money could be stretched out far enough to put in a new crop.

Grunting at the strain it put on his aching muscles, Lou rose slowly. "See you tomorrow, Sam."

"Sure," Nalley replied dully.

Lou looked back after he mounted Molly. Nalley would probably sit there for a long time tonight, staring blankly at nothing.

It wasn't quite dark when Lou arrived home. Swarms of grasshoppers covered everything as he rode onto his place. The two trees were bare, and the grass looked as though the season was midwinter.

A few of his chickens wandered through the front yard, occasionally picking at a grasshopper. He remembered how frantically the chickens had rushed about when the insect invasion first hit. Now, it looked as though they were too gorged to be interested in grasshoppers.

A worrisome thought struck him. After the grasshoppers left, would chickens and eggs get back to their normal taste? He hoped so. That might be his only food for quite a while.

He put Molly away and fed the horses. His supply of grain was dwindling. Lou shook his head. It wasn't going to last too long, and he didn't have the slightest idea where he could get more.

Lou didn't want to see the cornfield he had been so proud of. This was supposed to be a banner year, he thought in bitter resignation. This would certainly change matters from Celia's viewpoint. Lou expected a wave of sorrow to sweep over him, but oddly enough he was relieved. That physical attraction wasn't nearly as deep as he thought it would be.

He knew what he was going to do! Go to bed and sleep the clock around. At least, he could be thankful for that oblivion.

CHAPTER THIRTEEN

It was midmorning when Lou awakened. He sat on the side of the bed, stretching and yawning. How could he feel so tired after that much sleep?

He walked to the kitchen and looked at his reflection in the mirror. Rubbing his fingers across the stubbly growth on his chin, Lou muttered, "Damned, if you don't look like a wild man."

He went outside and drew water from the cistern, half afraid of seeing grasshoppers floating in the bucket, but, fortunately, the cistern lid was tight enough to keep them out. While he was at it, he might as well draw enough water to take a bath. God knew he needed it.

Lou heated enough water to half fill the washtub and added cold water from the cistern to bring the water to a comfortable temperature.

The water in the tub darkened in a hurry as he bathed. Lord, he was dirty. He left enough clean hot water with which to shave. Lou picked at a problem as he scraped the lather away. Those steers better be sold today before the price crumbled. He was sure the grasshoppers hadn't left any grass in the pasture, and his barn was almost empty of hay. Selling his cattle now would give him a fierce beating, but there was nothing else he could do.

A scowl was set on his face as he finished dressing. Once a man was down it seemed as though every kick in the world was aimed at him.

His head lifted as he heard that distressing sound. Only yesterday— He corrected that. It was the day before that he heard a similar sound. Oh God, he groaned, not more grasshoppers.

He ran out of the door and, for a moment, thought his fears were well grounded; it was another invasion of grasshoppers. Everywhere he looked the insects were on the wing.

"You came too late," he yelled at them. "The first ones got everything there was to eat."

Then he saw how wrong he was. As though on a prearranged signal, the grasshoppers on the ground were taking to their wings. Lou stared incredulously at them. The grasshoppers were leaving. He knew a surge of elation, then reality seized him. The grasshoppers' departure was coming too late.

The insects formed a cloud overhead, then drifted slowly toward the southeast. Lou watched the cloud until it was out of sight. He was sorry for the man that cloud dropped on.

"Some poor son of a bitch is going to get it," he muttered.

Lou couldn't still his faint hope as he walked toward his cornfield. Maybe the grasshoppers left while there was still something left.

He didn't have to go very deep into the field to kill his hope. As far as he could see, it looked as though he had planted short green broomsticks in rows. Here and there fragments of leaves had dropped to the ground, overlooked by the gorging insects. Lou wondered how many men looked at their ruined crops this morning.

"The poor bastards," he said aloud.

He walked to the pasture to confirm what he already knew. The grass was gone. He doubted he could find enough blades of grass to fill his hat. Sure, it would come back, but what were the cattle going to live on while they waited for the grass to grow. There was no doubt he had to sell his steers now, and several months too soon. This was the good year he had mentioned earlier to Nalley. Maybe Nalley was right in saying Lou jinxed it by saying anything favorable about the year.

"Damned nonsense," he muttered as he turned back to the barn. If he kept on with this kind of thinking, he would be taking the whole blame for what had happened.

Lou saddled Dandy without any trouble, for those annoying insects no longer crawled over his hide.

His face was remote as he rode into Russell. He had better look up Harry Edmonds before the cattle trader was deluged by other men in the same shape as Lou. Once that deluge started, the bottom of the cattle market would drop out. Lou might have to sell Dandy too, and that thought hurt. But he wasn't in a panic situation. There was no need to sell Dandy, but the stallion was another asset, and Lou would keep that thought in mind.

Edmonds was in his office. The heyday of Edmonds' business was gone. Once he had dealt in thousands of head of cattle when the trail herds came to Russell. Now Edmonds could count the deals he made each month on the fingers of one hand.

Edmonds sat behind his desk, staring gloomily at nothing. This office showed no sign of prosperity. Edmonds used to keep it as neat as a pin. Now it looked as though the floor hadn't been swept in months, and the windows were filthy.

"Hello, Lou," Edmonds said.

He was a small man with a bulbous nose and sad eyes. Lou could remember when Edmonds would walk into a saloon and buy a round of drinks for everybody there. That generosity, like so many other things, had vanished with the changing times. Outside of his father, Lou didn't know of another regular customer Edmonds had.

Lou sat down in a chair in front of the desk. "You get the hoppers here, Harry?"

Edmonds threw up his hands. "Did we? You should've heard the women squawk. Those grasshoppers made for real messy walking. 'Bout an hour ago, they picked up and flew away. They didn't leave a blade of grass or a leaf. They hit you?"

"Just about wiped me out," Lou replied.

Edmonds shook his head in sympathy. "Aw, I'm sorry to hear that."

Lou smiled bleakly. "It's a big boat. I suspect everybody in the county is in it." He made a slash with his hand. He hadn't come here to talk of his troubles. "Harry, I've got twenty-five head of steers. Are you interested in them?"

Edmonds squinted at him. "No feed?"

"That's about it."

"What shape are they in, Lou? What do they weigh?"

"I'd say close to six hundred." Maybe Lou was overstating their weight, but those steers had enough frame to carry eight hundred or eight hundred and fifty pounds. All they needed was a little more time and feed.

Edmonds figured on a piece of paper. "Lou, the best I can do is twenty dollars a head."

Lou stared at him in shocked disbelief. Edmonds' offer was less than Lou originally paid for the steers. On top of that, the steers had gained some weight.

"Why, damn it, Harry," he squalled. "I paid twenty-two a head for them."

Edmonds looked contrite. "I know what you're thinking, Lou. But it's the best I can do. You're lucky you decided to sell so quick. In a few days, every man in the county will be piling in here, begging me to take their cattle off their hands. You know what will happen to the price then."

Lou didn't quibble. Edmonds was an honest man. He was giving Lou all the market would bear. Edmonds had to make a few dollars, or there would be no sense staying in business.

Lou drew a deep breath. "Done." Oh, this year was pouring out good things in a flood.

"Be out this afternoon to look them over," Edmonds said. "If we're agreed, I'll bring a couple of boys with me to help drive them to town."

"Fine," Lou said. There was a bitter note to his voice. It wasn't fine at all. He hadn't expected to make a whole lot of money on those steers, but he hadn't expected to lose any, either.

Lou started to rise, then remembered something. "Harry, has Pa been in to see you?"

"Not for some time, Lou. Why?"

"With what's happened, I expected him to come in to talk to you."

Edmonds looked astonished. "You mean about selling out?" He drew a deep breath as though the enormity of the thought was too big for him to handle. "Hell, Lou, your father would never do that. He's spent too much time building up that herd."

"What's he going to do with them?" Lou asked quietly. "I know he hasn't got any grass left. Even if he could find and buy hay to feed them until the grass comes back, he couldn't afford it. Why, good God." His voice picked up passion. "What happened the last couple of days means he won't be able to put up any hay. How's he going to get through the winter?"

Edmonds shook his head in weary acceptance of the facts Lou laid before him. "It's a hell of a problem. I don't know what a lot of the farmers are going to do."

He stood as Lou rose and walked with him out of the door. His face lit up as he saw Dandy. "You ever decide to sell that horse, Lou, I'd make you a good offer. That stallion always took my eye."

Edmonds had made passes about buying Dandy before, and Lou had always turned him down. Maybe it would come down to where Lou would be forced to sell Dandy, but he hadn't reached that point yet. Dandy was one of the few luxuries Lou allowed himself.

"He's not for sale, Harry." Lou smiled to take the curtness out of his refusal.

"If you ever change your mind, let me know," Edmonds said.

"Sure," Lou replied. He untied Dandy and swung up into the saddle. Something Hiram told him long ago flashed through his mind. "Avoid selling on a distressed market. If you do, you'll take a beating every time."

Lou turned Hiram's words over in his mind as he headed for Arnold's store. It was still sound advice, but how in the hell could he avoid selling after what had happened?

He entered the store and was relieved to find no other customers there. It made it easier to say what he had in mind.

"Good morning, Hap," Lou said. "Bad the last couple of days, wasn't it?"

"We're still alive, ain't we?" Arnold asked cheerfully. "All I've done is listen to people complain about a few grasshoppers." He shook his head as though he couldn't understand that.

Arnold's cheerfulness irritated Lou. "A few grasshoppers," he said angrily. "Damn it, Hap. It's wiped out a lot of people. Is that something to be cheerful about?"

Arnold's face sobered. "That's bad, and I'm the first to admit it. But is it going to do them any good to hold their heads in their hands and sit around and moan? They're only wasting time they could be using to dig themselves out of the hole."

Lou had to laugh in spite of his low spirits. "You're something, Hap."

"Those aren't empty words, Lou. I've been in holes before, more times than I like to remember. But I've always managed to climb out. When you quit trying, you're dead."

Lou pursed his lips in reflective thought. Arnold had lived a lot longer than he had. Maybe he would be wise to think hard about what Arnold just said.

"Hap, I didn't come in to buy a thing today." Lou knew he was fumbling around, but the words he wanted to say wouldn't come out clean-cut. He guessed the only way to say it was to blurt it out.

"Hap, Sam Nalley was wiped out by the grasshoppers. He doesn't see how he can make it through until next year's crop. I owe him a lot. I can think of a dozen times when he reached out a hand to me when I needed it." He shook his head. There was no necessity in recounting those times to Arnold. Lou knew what they were. That was all that was needed.

Lou took a deep breath and let it all out. "I'm in better shape than Sam is. Can I make arrangements for his groceries to be charged to me until he gets back on his feet?"

Arnold looked speculatively at Lou. "Are you saying you want to pay for Nalley's groceries?"

Lou sighed in relief. It was all out in the open. "That's about it, Hap."

"You planning to tell Sam about this?"

"That's what I'm trying to avoid," Lou said in exasperation. He couldn't believe it, but Arnold was shaking his head.

Before Lou could speak Arnold asked, "How would you keep it from him? He's bound to find out sooner or later." At Lou's increasing frown, Arnold went doggedly on. "He's bound to find out. What you're planning is just fine. But Sam's a prideful man. He should be told. How do you think he will feel when somebody slaps him in the face with the fact he's accepting charity?"

"It's not charity," Lou said heatedly. "I told you—"

"I know you did, Lou. But you've got to give Sam a chance to accept or refuse. The worst thing we can do to a man is try to be sly about being kind."

Lou pulled at his ear lobe as he pondered what Arnold said. "Maybe you're right," he said slowly. "I'll talk it over with Sam." He grimaced at the prospects of telling Nalley what he had in mind. But Nalley had a family to think about. His present circumstances were too precarious for him to raise too much hell.

Arnold walked with Lou to the door. He slapped him on the shoulder. "You'll do, boy."

That was about as high praise as Lou would ever receive, and he couldn't help grinning. The grin was wiped off by the sight of the two people going down the other side of the street.

Seeing Herrick and Celia together hit Lou hard, and he tried to keep it from showing on his face. Seeing them like this didn't mean anything, he told himself to drown the stab of jealousy. But the moment meant something to Celia, he thought morosely. She was completely absorbed in what Herrick was saying. She looked up into Herrick's face and laughed. Lou's stab of jealousy was gone. He couldn't change things, if he wanted to. He would never be in worse shape to take on a wife.

When Lou faced Arnold again, his face was blank. But Arnold knew; it was in his eyes. The whole damned town knew how Lou had felt about her.

"A man can sure get himself in a mess," Lou muttered.

Arnold gripped Lou's arm and smiled. "Never heard of one who didn't." He let Lou take a couple of steps before he called after him, "You let me know what arrangements you make with Sam."

"I'll do that," Lou returned.

The bank was only a half block down the street, and Lou led Dandy. He had one more errand to do; he had to talk to Welles Parnell. That could be the toughest job of all.

Lou did some mental figuring as he walked toward the bank. If Edmonds bought the steers, and Lou could see no reason why he shouldn't, that should amount to five hundred dollars. Added to what he already had in the bank, he would have just a little under a thousand dollars. That was a sizable sum, but he was scared of being able to stretch it to include Nalley's expenses and his own, plus the planting of a new crop. He scowled ferociously as he thought of all the glowing pictures he had painted for Celia. He shook his head in resignation. That didn't matter now. He waited for the agony to sweep over him, and it didn't come. Lou guessed he was learning to accept the inevitable.

His mind went back to the problem of putting in a brand-new crop. He didn't know whether or not he would need new implements; he had no idea of what wheat seed would cost. Now Lou was really scared. He felt as though he looked into a black pool that he must dive into, and he didn't know how deep that pool was.

Lou was frowning as he stepped inside the bank. Another five hundred dollars should give him all the margin he needed to be able to take a free breath. He should be able to borrow that much. His farm should be more than enough collateral for Parnell to consider lending the money to him. Just the thought of Parnell's possible refusal made Lou physically ill. He tried to shake all the terrifying doubts from his mind. The longer he stood and looked at that dark pool without making a move, the harder it would be to take the plunge.

He sucked in a ragged breath as he approached the teller's cage. Welles could be a tough one to handle. Lou knew the animosity Welles felt for him. Plus that, there was the grasshopper plague. That could make Welles much more reluctant to listen to reason.

Lou drew another breath. He would never know how deep that pool was until he dived in.

CHAPTER FOURTEEN

"Hello, Charley," Lou said.

Mills's eyes were evasive. "Hello, Lou," he mumbled.

He remembers the comments I made about his boss, Lou thought. The extent of Mills's loyalty amazed Lou. The man is even afraid to talk to me.

Lou kept his voice pleasant. "Is Welles in?"

Mills's darting glance at the closed office door told Lou Parnell was in there, but Mills was afraid to say so.

"Come on, Charley." Lou couldn't keep the edge out of his voice. "He's in. I want to see him."

Mills couldn't keep the trembling out of his hands, and he still wouldn't look at Lou. "I know he's awfully busy today, Lou. I'm sure he hasn't time to see you."

"You go and ask him anyway, Charley. I've got business with him. It won't take long."

Lou grinned at Mills's covert glance. Mills was worried about the definition of that word "business."

"I'm not looking for trouble, Charley. I just want to talk to Welles."

How badly Mills wanted to refuse. Lou watched him try to find enough backbone to say "No," but evidently Mills didn't have it, for he sighed and said, "I'll see, Lou. I don't know what he's going to say."

Mills turned and crossed to the office door. He was worried, and the sag of his shoulders bore mute testimony to his fears.

Lou fell in behind him. He expected Mills to turn his head and tell him to wait, but if Mills knew Lou was there, he gave no sign.

Lou wanted to snort in disgust at Mills's feeble tap on the door. Hell, that couldn't be heard two feet.

But Lou was wrong, for an impatient voice called, "Yes. What is it?"

Mills opened the door less than four inches. Lou could see only Parnell's shoulder and left arm.

"Somebody out here to see you, Mr. Parnell," Mills said in a shaky voice.

"Who is it?" Parnell demanded.

"Lou Manard, sir." Mills's voice was little more than a whisper.

Lou heard a small thud. It could be the sound of an angry fist smashing down on a desk.

"Tell him no," Parnell shouted.

Lou reached over Mills's shoulder and pushed at the door, tearing it out of Mills's hands. He stepped around Mills and entered the office. He heard Mills's frightened squawk behind him but ignored it.

"I have to see you, Welles," Lou said. "This is a matter of business."

Parnell's face was turning purple, and his malevolent eyes raked Lou. "We've got nothing to talk about," he spluttered.

Lou kept his face composed, though there was anger behind that smooth facade. He guessed he was foolish to come in here, but he hadn't believed Parnell would carry a grudge this far. He crossed the office and sat down in a chair without an invitation.

"Never heard of a day when you'd turn down business, Welles," he said evenly.

Parnell half rose from his chair. For a moment, Lou wondered if Parnell was going to try to throw him out physically.

No, he thought, as Parnell settled back into his chair. Evidently, the memory of their last clash was sharp and vivid in Parnell's mind, for he breathed hard.

Parnell looked past Lou and yelled, "Charley, get out of here."

Lou heard the door close softly, and he could imagine Mills scurrying away.

"What do you want?" Parnell growled.

"I came to see about a loan on my place," Lou said quietly. Oh God, how it hurt to say those words.

Parnell looked startled, then his eyes turned crafty. "How much did you have in mind?"

Lou couldn't believe it, but Parnell was listening. "I need five hundred dollars. I think you know my place is clear."

Parnell seemed to get an immense pleasure from hearing Lou asking for a favor. "The grasshoppers cleaned you out?"

The muscles along Lou's jaw bunched. How Parnell was enjoying seeing Lou squirm.

"You know they did," Lou said levelly. "You own several farms. Yours didn't come through any better."

Parnell leaned back in his chair and clasped his hands over his stomach. "That's true," he admitted. "But I seem to be in better shape than you. I don't have to borrow any money."

Lou's grip on his temper was slipping. "I guess that's a no, isn't it?"

"You catch on quick," Parnell said mockingly. "Hell, you can come out of it without my help. All you have to do is to plant your damned wheat."

Lou got slowly to his feet. If he didn't get out of here, he would lunge across that desk and drag Parnell over it. That would really fix him good, wouldn't it? Briner would slam him into jail so fast Lou wouldn't know how he got there.

"You're really a stupid man, Welles," Lou said coldly. "You couldn't see anything, if your nose was rubbed in it."

Parnell's face turned a choleric red, and he looked as though he was having difficulty getting his breath.

"You get out of here." Parnell's voice rose on each word until he was screaming.

"I'm going," Lou drawled. He had a lot more he wanted to say, but they wouldn't gain him a thing. He stalked to the door, turned there, and pityingly shook his head. Lou forced out a laugh, and he hoped it rang true.

The laugh was better than any words, for it drove Parnell wild. If he didn't simmer down, he was going to have a stroke.

Mills was waiting for Lou just outside his cage, and his face was worried. "Did you get what you wanted?"

"No," Lou admitted. All he had gotten out of this visit was a certain amount of satisfaction. A man couldn't feed his belly or build much future with that. Lou frowned at the old man. Were the voices in Parnell's office that loud, or had Mills put his ear up against the door? Age seemed to give a man the prerogative to pry into everything. Lou kept a firm grip on his temper.

"It doesn't matter, Charley," he said quietly.

"But it does," Mills insisted. "You came in here looking for trouble. You raked up the old argument. You'd have been smarter if you came in to apologize." He had that smug, self-satisfied look of a man who knows he's right. "I tried to warn you Welles didn't want to talk to you. But you went right ahead."

Lou's grip on his temper was slipping. "Back away, Charley," he said heatedly. "I don't know how much you heard, but you've got it all wrong. I had a legitimate reason to talk to Welles." He grimaced and spread his palms. "If you heard enough, you know Welles is an unforgiving man. My God," he exploded. "You've worked for him long enough. I thought you'd know that better than anyone else."

Mills stubbornly shook his head. "Did you expect him to want to talk to you?" he cried. "After what you did to him?"

"Oh, for God's sake," Lou said in exasperation. "Go in there and tell him how loyal you are. You're not doing any good with me."

Mills started to say something else, and Lou cut him short. His brief flare of temper was gone, and Lou said in disgusted resignation, "Oh, shut up." He turned and walked toward the door.

He untied Dandy and mounted, hesitating for a moment. Edmonds said he would be out to look at the steers this afternoon. Lou had time to talk to Doyle before Edmonds arrived. He knew he should take this opportunity of seeing Celia; to tell her that everything was changed, but he couldn't force himself into facing her right now. Those would be bitter words to say, to admit that he had failed in all his promises to her. He shrugged. He could see her another time.

"Let's go, Dandy," he said. He hadn't gained much this morning. Sure, he wasn't any worse off than before he walked into the bank. It would have been nice, he thought wistfully, if Parnell had been agreeable. That five hundred dollars would have made the cushion he needed. It didn't alter Lou's plans in the least. He was going ahead just as he figured, but the margin had been cut closer than he wanted.

Lou rode up to his father's house, and for a moment, he thought no one was around. He walked up onto the porch and called, "Anybody around?"

"In here," Doyle answered. Lou winced at the tone of the voice. It sounded heavy and depressed. Lou guessed Doyle had every right to that tone after what had happened to him.

Lou opened the door and stepped inside. Doyle was sprawled out in a chair, and he looked utterly beaten. A bottle sat beside his chair, and a half-filled glass was in his hand.

"There's a glass in the kitchen," Doyle said.

Lou shook his head. "You think that's going to solve anything?"

He expected a flare of temper from Doyle, but instead Doyle answered dully, "It keeps a man from thinking."

Lou thought of Hap Arnold's words. Doyle should have talked to

Arnold. Maybe he wouldn't be sitting in his hole instead of trying to find some way to dig out.

Doyle drained his glass and refilled it. Lou's weighing look got to him, and he said, "Goddamn it, don't sit there judging me. Do you know what's happened?"

"I should," Lou said calmly. "It wiped out this year for me, too."

Doyle glared at him, then took a long swallow.

"Keep up that pace, and you won't have to worry much about anything," Lou said sardonically.

He braced himself for the explosion that should bring and was surprised it didn't come. He's taken one hell of a spiritual beating, Lou thought. He pitied his father, but he wasn't going to get down and wallow in the same misery.

After a long silence, Lou asked, "What are you going to do?"

"What in the hell am I supposed to do?" Doyle growled. "Those goddamned things wiped out every blade of grass. I couldn't find enough grass to fill my hat."

Lou nodded. Hadn't he gone through the same experience, though not on such a disastrous scale.

"You can't hang on to the cattle," Lou pointed out.

Doyle stared at him, and Lou saw life return to his eyes. "I guess you've got an answer," Doyle snapped. Even this antagonism was better than the numbed acceptance of a few moments ago.

"There might be," Lou said. "You could sell the cattle."

Doyle looked as though Lou had struck him across the face. "If that's the best you can come up with, keep your ideas to yourself," he choked.

"Can you think of anything better?" Lou asked practically. "You've got to start haying right away, or you're going to have hungry cattle on your hands."

Doyle breathed hard. "I've got some hay the hoppers didn't get. The grass will come back."

That could be true, Lou admitted. Maybe his father had some hay ahead, but it wouldn't be enough. Once the cattle got ahead of the grass, it seemed it took forever for it to show any growth.

"Maybe you can get by right now," Lou said. "But what about the winter hay? You can't plan on enough growth to put up much hay."

Doyle's groan told how his soul was wracked. It was an eloquent admission of how all this same reasoning had gone through his tortured mind.

Then Doyle's face turned savage, and Lou thought he was going to throw the glass at him. "How would you solve this?" he yelled.

"I'd sell the cattle just as fast as I could get them to market," Lou replied.

It took Doyle a couple of tries before he could get his words out. "Of all the goddamned fool ideas. Do you know what that would cost me?"

Lou nodded. "I should. I just sold twenty-five head of steers. I took a beating. You'd take one, too."

That should bring Doyle roaring up out of his chair. Instead, he sagged back into it, and his face went gray, his lips pinched.

"I've spent all my life in this business," he said in a barely audible tone. "And you suggest something like that."

Lou was filled with sympathy for his father, but he didn't let it show. Sympathy wasn't going to do anybody any good. Doyle had to face hard facts.

"I know what you're saying," Lou said. "You wanted to be one of the biggest ranchers in Kansas. You couldn't be the biggest because you didn't have enough land." He raised a hand to check Doyle's outburst. "Can't you see, Pa? Even that dream has been ripped out of your hands. You've got to think of something else. You've got two thousand acres. If you can't raise cattle on it, maybe you can raise wheat. Why good Lord! That much land could make you one of the biggest wheat growers in Kansas."

Doyle bristled like an angry hedgehog. "Are you saying I should be a damned farmer?" he howled.

"Something like that," Lou said and grinned. "They've got a new wheat in western Kansas that's doing well. Maybe that's what this country was supposed to grow in the first place. Can't you see, Pa?" Lou didn't try to hide the pleading in his voice. "The farmers tried to raise corn, and the drought last year and the plague this year pretty well knocked that idea out of their heads. They've got to turn to something else."

Lou leaned forward, his face intent. "All of us are only trying to make a living. What difference does it make which road we take to reach that goal?"

Doyle shook his head, a slow, stubborn gesture. "That's the damnedest fool thing I ever heard you say. Why, I wouldn't even consider it."

Lou stood and shrugged. "It's your land, Pa. You can do what you please with it. For me, I'd rather turn to something new that has a promise than stand around and watch my cattle slowly starve to death."

Doyle didn't respond, and Lou sighed. Maybe some of his own stubbornness came from Doyle. That trait was all right to an extent. But let it run without some thinking behind it, and it could mean the final ruin of a man.

Lou walked to the door and looked back. Doyle hadn't even turned his head. Lou could feel the refusal coming from him in tangible waves.

"It's your decision, Pa. I just wanted you to know there's another way."

Doyle sat there, staring straight ahead. To hell with him, Lou thought in rising wrath. He curbed the feeling. This was a violent change. It would take Doyle time to adjust to a new idea.

"All right, Pa," Lou said. "I'll be seeing you again."

He closed the door behind him. He didn't expect an answer.

CHAPTER FIFTEEN

On the way home Lou thought of his talk with Doyle. Could it have turned out differently, if he had handled it better? Lou doubted it.

"He's one hard-headed man, Dandy," Lou muttered. Doyle was a grown man; he made his own decisions and however they turned out was no burden on anyone else's shoulders. No matter how much strength Lou put into that thought, he couldn't keep the worry from plaguing him.

He had barely put Dandy away in the barn when Edmonds arrived. Edmonds didn't say much, but Lou sensed a dubiousness in his manner. Oh God, Lou thought in quick dismay. He's regretted his buy. He swore at himself. He was turning into a worry wart. He didn't need a signed piece of paper to know that Edmonds would go through with what he said.

Edmonds had two teen-agers with him to help drive the steers back to town. Lou knew both of them, and he said, "Hello, Jim, Andy." This was a happy time of life for them. Tomorrow cast no shadow that they could see.

"The steers are out in the pasture, Harry," Lou said. "It's just a short distance. No sense in me getting saddled up."

"I'll walk with you," Edmonds offered. "I do too little of that lately."

Edmonds led his horse, and the two boys followed. Lou kept casting covert glances at Edmonds. Something was bothering him, and the worry started anew in Lou. Had Edmonds ridden out here just to tell him the deal was off? Lou put a hard hand on his rising panic. That would really put the finishing touches on a day rapidly turning sour. It can't be, he argued with himself. He brought Jim and Andy with him, didn't he?

"Something troubled you, Harry?" Lou asked.

Edmonds sighed. "I guess I didn't realize how hard the county has been hit. I had a half-dozen offers to buy cattle after you left. I had to turn them down."

Lou felt his neck growing hot. Edmonds sounded as though Lou had tricked him. "Do you want to call the deal off?" he asked stiffly.

Edmonds chuckled. "Don't go stiff-necked on me. I'm here, ain't I?"

He walked a few more paces, wrestling with his thoughts. "You were smart to move when you did, Lou."

That made Lou feel better. "Harry, I rode out and talked to Doyle after I left you."

"Got him in a bind, hasn't it?" Edmonds asked.

"He doesn't know which way to turn. It's driving him wild."

"Is he thinking of selling his cattle?"

"Not right now," Lou said flatly. "Even with an ideal fall I doubt he'll be able to put up enough hay to get through."

Edmonds grunted sympathetic understanding. "Sometimes a man gets so hemmed in he doesn't know which way to turn."

"I advised him to sell," Lou said quietly.

Edmonds' face showed doubt. "Couldn't be a worse time, even if he found buyers. If he sold out, what's he going to do?"

Lou drew a quick breath. Edmonds was an old cattleman; he might greet Lou's words with the same hooting disbelief as other people had shown. "He's still got the land, Harry. More than anybody has for miles around. He'd get something out of the cattle, wouldn't he?" Lou went on. "Enough to put in wheat."

"Ah," Edmonds said reflectively. "Wheat."

His tone surprised Lou, for there was no derision in it.

Edmonds' glance weighed Lou. "You suggest wheat to him?"

Lou nodded. "Yes, because that's what I'm going to put in. I can't see any other way out."

"How did Doyle take it?"

Lou grimaced at the memory. "Hard."

"I can imagine," Edmonds said dryly. "It's changing his entire way of life. At his age that's hard to accept. Hell, I don't know what I'm going to do myself." He spat on the ground. "You think he's going to listen to what you said?"

"I don't know. He sure hadn't accepted the idea when I left."

Edmonds spat again. "Some of us are like cattle. We can't see a gate until we're driven through it. Find one for me, will you?"

"You ready to plant wheat?" Lou asked and grinned.

Edmonds shuddered. "I'm not driven that hard yet. Come around in a few weeks. Maybe I'll be ready to listen to you."

Lou opened the gate to the pasture. The steers were just ahead of them.

Edmonds turned his head and called to Jim and Andy. "You two hell raisers take it easy until I decide what to do."

Again that stab of fear laced through Lou. Edmonds sounded as though he was still undecided about taking the cattle.

Edmonds tied his horse to the gate and walked with Lou toward the steers. The steers were restless, but they didn't break. Lou could swear they'd gone down since he last looked at them.

"Not in the best shape, are they, Lou?" Edmonds asked.

"They're hungry," Lou said shortly. "I told you that."

Edmonds grinned at Lou's frown. "Don't go searching for any cuss words. The price still stands. I didn't expect them to look any better." He raised his voice. "Hey, Andy, Jim. Let's start them moving."

The two kids went at the job of getting the steers started toward the gate with the usual overzealousness of youth. They dug their heels in their horses' flanks and whooped at the top of their voices.

"Goddamn it," Edmonds roared. "Take it easy. Do you want to run all the weight off of them?"

The rebuke put an abashed look on the boys' faces, and they slowed their horses' pace to a walk.

Edmonds looked at Lou and shook his head. "Wish I had the piss and vinegar to go at a job like they do."

He moved out of the gate and watched the steers go through. Lou felt a small pang as he looked at the steers. Not too many days ago he was filled with the pride of ownership whenever he looked at them. He could no longer experience that feeling. That was all done now, and dwelling on it wouldn't do him any good.

"Better keep those kids down," Lou said steadily, "or they'll be running them again." Walking those steers to town would be a long, dreary job to those kids.

"If they do, I'll kick their butts off," Edmonds said crossly. He counted out twenty-five twenty-dollar bills in Lou's hand. "I wonder how long I'll be able to keep on doing this," he said morosely. "I'm not so sure which one of us made the best deal, Lou."

"Under the circumstances, probably neither of us, Harry," Lou replied. He sincerely hoped that Edmonds made a few dollars out of his purchase. He would hate to see men like Edmonds driven out of business.

"We'll see," Edmonds grunted. He started to swing up, then paused. "Haven't changed your mind about selling Dandy?"

"Not yet," Lou replied. "I promise I'll give you first crack at him, if I do."

Edmonds mounted and lifted his hand in farewell. Lou watched him until he was out of sight. He felt restless and lonely at the same time. He didn't have a damned thing left on the farm he could turn into cash, unless it was Dandy and the two heavy draft animals. He swore at himself for the frightened thinking. He wasn't up against it yet, but a man did like to wallow in his misery.

He squinted at the sky. There were two hours of daylight left, and he could use the time to ride over and talk to Nalley.

Don't go stubborn on me, Sam, he thought as he walked to the barn and resaddled Dandy. He had talked to enough stubborn men this day.

Nalley sat on the porch, staring into space when Lou rode into the yard. Lou could almost swear Nalley hadn't moved since he left him last night.

He swung down, tethered Dandy, walked up onto the porch and dropped into a chair. "How's it going, Sam?"

Nalley's eyes rested briefly on Lou, and there was a bitterness in them. The look said that was a stupid question.

"Been doing any thinking over what we talked about last night, Sam?"

Nalley sighed. "I've had a million thoughts. None of them worth a damn." He managed a twisted smile. "Know any place a beat-up old farmer can hire out for a few dollars? I'd work cheap."

Nalley should have talked to Hap Arnold this morning, Lou thought. If Nalley hasn't actually quit, he's beginning to die. Maybe it was only normal, and Lou curbed his impatience with Nalley.

"Sam, the way I see it, there's no other road left open to us." Lou rocked for a moment. It looked as though Nalley wasn't going to respond.

"What am I going to start with?" Nalley finally said. "I told you last night I'm broke, or closer to it than I like to think about." Indignation strengthened his voice. "Here you come around prattling about putting in a new crop. You tell me with what."

"Maybe I can, Sam." It was going to be real hard to talk to Nalley today. "You know those steers I had?" He rushed on, not waiting for Nalley's nod. "Edmonds bought them for five hundred dollars."

"You're one of the lucky ones," Nalley said heavily. "I can't think of a damned thing I've got to sell."

"Maybe both of us are lucky, Sam. I think the steers brought enough to put in both crops." Last night, Nalley had been against wheat, and by the rock-hard set of his face, he hadn't changed.

Lou searched for another argument. "Damn it, Sam. Wheat will be harvested months before corn. Doesn't that mean anything to you? You'd have a cash crop long before you could even think of harvesting corn."

Nalley's eyes were smoky with resentment. "You've got it all figured out, haven't you? Now you tell me what I'm going to live on until the wheat harvest comes. That's not even counting the money it will take to put the wheat in."

Lou might be arousing Nalley's wrath, but it had to be said now, or he might never find the courage again.

"I did some thinking on that too, Sam. I didn't have too much money in the bank, but with the steer money I think there's enough for both of us to go ahead."

Nalley must have gotten a glimmer of what Lou was proposing, for his eyes were beginning to burn. Lou rushed on; he didn't dare let Nalley interrupt. "I talked to Hap Arnold today. You go ahead and buy all the groceries you need. I'll take care of them." There, it was all out, and Lou waited anxiously for Nalley's reaction.

Nalley sucked hard for breath, and his face paled, making the small scar on a cheekbone stand out vividly. He stared at Lou, and outrage twisted his features.

"I don't appreciate that, Lou." Nalley tried to say it calmly, but his voice kept rising. "Why, goddamn it. Did I come whining to you that I wanted charity?"

The vehemence of his words momentarily shocked Lou. "Hold it, Sam," he begged. "This isn't charity as you call it. I'll keep track of every cent. You can pay me back when you harvest your wheat."

Nalley's face kept darkening, and Lou said frantically, "You're looking at things all wrong, Sam. I remember quite a few things you did for me. I'm just trying to cut down on my debt to you."

Nalley shook his head violently. "An entirely different thing," he snapped. "That was only neighborly help. I didn't try to cram money down your throat." He cleared his throat and managed to get his voice under control. "Lou, I'm going to forget you ever mentioned it."

Before Lou could reply there was a rush of feet behind them. He turned his head and saw Maude flying out of the door.

Lou groaned. She was mad; it was written all over her face. She must have been listening at the window behind Nalley. She'd heard enough to really set her off. Now, he had two angry people on his hands.

He started to say something, and Maude cried, "You stay out of this, Lou Manard."

Maude planted herself before her father. Her hands were on her hips, and her head was cocked to one side. Lou couldn't remember ever seeing her this angry.

"I'm ashamed of you, Pa, talking to Lou like that." Her words came so fast they jammed together. "Don't try to fall back on your poor, hurt pride."

Lou let out a careful breath. He could relax, for Maude was after Sam, not him. He wanted to grin, but he knew he didn't dare let it show. Who would ever have thought Maude had a temper like this?

Nalley started to speak, and Maude cut him short. "Do you know what's wrong with you, Pa? You're a selfish man. You want to do things for other people. But you don't want them to know the same pleasure."

Nalley's face clouded, and he roared, "Just a damned minute."

"Don't get your back up at me," Maude said hotly. "You know it's true. Lou wants to get out from under the burden he feels he owes you, but your stiff-necked pride won't let you accept. He expects you to pay the money back, every damned cent of it. All he's doing is waiting a little while for it."

She glanced at Lou and ducked her head but not before he saw the glistening of tears in her eyes; angry tears. He smiled at her in open admiration. She could administer a verbal lashing about as well as anybody he knew.

"Maude," Lou said softly.

She angrily brushed at her eyes before she looked at him.

"I tried to tell him that, Maude," Lou went on. "But you said it better. Damn it," he said mournfully. "I thought Sam and I were good-enough friends that we could talk about anything. I guess I was wrong."

"Pa hasn't learned that giving isn't a one-way road," Maude said scathingly. She spoke as though Nalley wasn't anywhere around. "When that road turns and comes back, it's called receiving. That makes the complete road."

Nalley blinked at Maude. The outrage had faded from his face. "You're not too old to paddle," he said, but there was no anger in his voice.

"I wish I could say the same for you," Maude cried. She whirled and ran back into the house.

Both men rocked in silence. Nalley finally said, "I just found I don't know her at all. Why, she's got a temper like an annoyed bumblebee."

"She speaks her mind," Lou said cautiously. "It's not a bad trait, particularly when she's right." It startled Lou to realize Maude had given him a new outlook on several things.

Nalley studied his work-gnarled knuckles. "She cleared up my eyesight pretty good."

"Mine too," Lou said in a wondering voice. He wasn't ready to explain that remark, even to himself. He had seen something in Maude he didn't know existed.

"Lou, I got a little money. Not much. It won't carry me long. What I'm trying to say is that it sort of wipes out the fear in a man when he realizes he's not alone."

A long, soft breath escaped Lou. There was no use to thrash this matter longer; it was all settled.

"We could fall on our faces, Sam," he warned.

"I've been there before," Nalley said stoutly.

Lou grinned at him, feeling the warm flow of the bond between them. "But we won't, Sam. I feel it in my bones."

"Is that feeling as good as money in the bank?" Nalley asked, but his eyes were twinkling.

"You can write a check on it," Lou said. "Speaking of money in the bank, I'd better deposit what Edmonds gave me today. I don't like to have it laying around the house."

"It wouldn't be smart," Nalley said gravely. "Hell, if I knew where you put it, I'd be after it myself."

"That's what I'm afraid of," Lou said and chuckled. "Sam, how's your plow?"

"Dull. I didn't plan on using it until next year."

"Mine could stand some sharpening, too," Lou said. "We'd better get both of them ready." At Nalley's surprised look, he went on, "If we put in wheat, we have to turn our timetable all around. We'll be planting before September is out. We've got a lot of plowing to do."

Nalley nodded slowly. "How much land do you think we should plow, Lou?"

Lou didn't know for sure. That depended upon so many things; particularly how the money held out. "All we can, Sam. Before next year's over, maybe we'll change all of Kansas' farming habits."

"By God, I'd like to be one of the leaders instead of a follower," Nalley said wistfully. "I'll come by and pick you up in the morning."

"I'll be waiting." Lou felt fine. He and Nalley were in full harmony again.

"You'll stay for supper," Nalley said. He made it a statement instead of a question.

Lou wanted to; he wanted to look at Maude again. But this new thought was so startling and new that he wanted time to fully examine it.

"I'll pass it up this time, Sam. There's still a little daylight left. I've got to take that plowshare off and save time in the morning."

Nalley got to his feet as Lou rose. "Maybe I'd better be doing the same thing."

Lou shook Nalley's hand. This wasn't the beaten man he had seen sitting on the porch. This was a man with hope.

" 'Night, Sam," Lou said and went down the steps.

CHAPTER SIXTEEN

Parnell's hand shook as he laid down the pencil. The inward fear was a rising tide, threatening to engulf him. He had been over these figures a dozen times, and the damning answer was always the same. His books showed he was close to fifteen thousand dollars short. He wanted to throw back his head and scream at the unfairness of it all. He had tried to buy up too much land, and the grasshopper plague had ruined him. Values were dropping all around him, and each day saw a new low. He had believed in Kansas land, and he could prove where that money went. But that wouldn't satisfy the bank examiners. They would look at him with cold, unrelenting eyes, and each new figure they jotted down would fix the accusation in them.

Parnell got up and paced back and forth across the room.

Think, damn you, he admonished himself. There had to be some way he could get his hands on ready money. He groaned hollowly at the futility of that thought. The bank had money outstanding, but it couldn't be recalled on an instant's notice. Many of those loans were long term, but maybe some of them were close enough to due date that he could collect a few of them now.

Parnell hurried back to his desk and feverishly began figuring again.

His eyes were sick with despair as he looked at the final total. It wasn't anywhere near the figure he needed.

Parnell leaned back in his chair, trying to quiet his churning stomach. He thought he would vomit. Don't panic, he told himself. He had assets. All he needed was to find a way to convert them into cash.

He raised his head angrily at the tapping on his door. He knew who that was. Only he and Mills were in the bank at this hour of the night.

"What is it, Charley?" he asked impatiently.

Mills opened the door and thrust a cautious face inside. "Is there anything else I can do for you, Mr. Parnell?"

Parnell wanted to scream at him, and with difficulty he curbed his words. Mills didn't have any worries, he thought bitterly. He collected his salary every week.

"No, that's all, Charley," he said wearily. He had kept Mills busy all evening, collecting the papers and ledgers he needed.

"I just wanted to remind you, Mr. Parnell, that the bank examiners are supposed to be here next week."

"You doddering old fool," Parnell screamed. "Don't you think I know that?"

Mills paled before the fury on Parnell's face. He backed out of the door and closed it softly behind him.

The fear was rising in Parnell again, rising in a solid knot in his throat, blocking his breathing. Oh God! He could see his big mistake now. He wanted to be a big man too fast. If he had only been content to take it a little slower . . . The self-accusation was too bitter, and he tried to temper it. All of his plans would have worked out, if nature hadn't conspired against him. Only this week, two of his land deals fell through because the falling values scared people.

Parnell beat his hands together in frustration. All he needed was time to work out of this bind, but he didn't know where he was going to find that time.

Parnell felt as though he was gagging, and he stood. If he didn't get out of this room, he would go crazy.

"You need a drink," he muttered. Maybe a drink or two would clear his head, and he could think again.

He picked up his hat and walked over to a mirror to adjust its set on his head. God! He looked like a disaster. He smiled bitterly. That was too accurate a description.

He walked out of the office and closed the door behind him. If only that closed door could shut out the thoughts in his mind.

"You're not dead yet, Welles," he said, trying to put some life into his voice. "You've still got time."

He locked the front door behind him. He wished he could leave it open for somebody to walk in and clean out the safe. A good robbery right now might be just the thing to get him off the hook. A startled gleam flashed in his eyes. That could be the solution! If such a thing happened, the loss could always be reported to be far greater than it was.

Parnell breathed harder as he headed for Storhmier's. The only thing he needed now was to find that robber.

2

Storhmier stopped by Celia's piano. She was playing, and he tapped her on the shoulder to get her attention.

"You're wasting your time," he said and swept an arm about the nearly empty room. Only four customers were in the place, and this was as crowded as it had been all evening. Business hadn't been any better on previous evenings.

Celia rubbed her fingers to erase the ache from them. She was so bored she could scream, only playing because there was nothing else to do. She was used to admiring men listening to her; she needed the sound of their voices and the drinks they bought her.

"It hardly pays to open the door," she said in a quick petulant rush of temper.

Storhmier's little eyes surveyed her, and he said softly, "Maybe you've got an idea there."

Celia knew a quick panic. Sometimes her mouth was too big for her own good. "You know I didn't mean that, Quincy."

"You better hadn't," Storhmier said grimly. "Or it'll go hard on a lot of us."

The panic kept rising in Celia. If Storhmier closed his doors, she would be out of a job. It wouldn't be the first time such a thing had happened in her life, but then she had the resiliency of youth, and she bounded higher and harder each time she was slammed down. Then she could shrug and go out and find another job. Now, she felt suddenly much older and so much more weary. The thought of more travel with no definite destination wiped out her stomach, leaving only a cold, empty void.

She pressed back the swelling terror and smiled at Storhmier. "It'll get better, Quincy. This is just a slow day."

She had never seen the rage flood so quickly over Storhmier's face. Ordinarily, he was a calm, placid man, but tonight something had aroused him. Celia searched her mind for something she might have said to anger him so, and for the life of her, she could find nothing offensive in her remarks.

"If you're so damned smart, tell me where people are going to get the money. Why, damn it," Storhmier raged, "don't you realize what's happened?"

She smiled at him, trying to soften his mood. "Nothing unusual I know of, Quincy." Her mind fastened on something, and her face brightened. Surely, Storhmier couldn't mean the grasshopper invasion, but it was all she could think of.

"If you mean the grasshoppers, Quincy, that's all over." She shuddered at the memory. She had made only one brief foray into the streets, then scurried back into Storhmier's. She could still feel the crushing of all those little bodies, and the slimy smear on her shoes was more than she could bear. She hadn't ventured out again until she was sure the grasshoppers were gone. Why in the world would Storhmier be so worked up about grasshoppers?

Storhmier didn't look so angry now. Instead, his fat face looked like a mass of stale dough. He shook his head and said, "What do you use for a brain, Celia? Those grasshoppers are gone, but what they did to this country will last for a long time. Along with everything else they ate, those grasshoppers ate up most of the people's money. At least, the chance of making more. Everybody is broke." He turned his head and scowled about the room. "I'm surprised to see this many people here tonight."

"Ah, they'll be back," Celia said lightly. "This lull won't last long. Men will find money for drinks and a little pleasure. I know," she said firmly. "It'll always happen that way."

Storhmier looked at her as though she was beyond comprehension. "You don't know a damned thing you're talking about. You've never seen anything like this happen before. Men have to find eating money first before they start thinking of pleasure."

He looked around the room again. "Do you know what they're buying in here tonight? A few beers. Nothing else. How long do you think I can keep open on a few beers?" His grin was a ghastly paradox. "Maybe this will delight Briner and the good people of the town. All of them have been wanting to see me closed down for a long time."

Now, he really frightened Celia, but she refused to give way to panic. Her face brightened. "You just got another customer. Welles Parnell just came in. Surely, things couldn't be as bad as you think they are, or he wouldn't be here."

Storhmier watched Parnell walk up to the bar, and his eyes were reflective. "Now, what's he doing here? Welles is well known as a frugal man with a dime. Nobody can accuse him of spending money recklessly." Some of the despair left his face. "I'd better go have a talk with him. Maybe he knows something I don't."

He started away, then stopped. "No use knocking yourself out, Celia. Take a little time off." He waddled away toward Parnell.

Celia rose and walked to a table. It was a relief to get away from that hard bench. Ordinarily, she wouldn't be alone for over a minute or two. But tonight nobody seemed in the mood to vie for the pleasure of buying her a drink. She wanted to bawl in her frustration.

Herrick came over and stood looking down at her.

"What are you staring at?" she asked in a quick flare of temper.

"At somebody who looks as though she doesn't enjoy being alone," Herrick said sardonically. He sat down and leaned toward her. "Your hick never came back, did he, Celia?"

She felt the heat of anger in her cheeks. "That's none of your business, is it?"

Herrick grinned, more sure of himself. "Your disappointment's showing, Celia. You should have figured he wouldn't be back. The hoppers wiped him out along with all the others."

The panic threatened to engulf her. If she had ever seriously considered Lou, that was all over now.

"That should worry you too, Phil," she said acidly. "The same thing may have wiped out your job, too. Quincy sounded like he was getting desperate."

Herrick frowned as he looked around the room. "He has every right to be. He's not doing enough business to pay him to open the doors."

"Doesn't that bother you?" Celia asked furiously.

Bitter frustration flashed across his face. "Hell yes, it bothers me." If these doors closed, he knew he would never see Celia again. That thought twisted his guts.

"Do you know what I'd do if I had the money, Celia?" he asked. "I'd take you to New Orleans. You've never been there?" She shook her head, and he went on, "That's where you belong, not in this one-horse town. I've been there. I can just see you in your own carriage, driving up to the finest restaurants. Every woman there would be green with envy at the way men's eyes would follow you."

"Big dreams," she said sullenly. Herrick had less money than she, and from what Storhmier hinted, both their jobs were in jeopardy.

Herrick's crestfallen face touched her, and she stretched out a hand to cover his. "You're sweet," she said softly. "I wish you did have the money."

3

"How are things going, Welles?" Storhmier asked Parnell.

"Never finer," Parnell boomed. His eyes were fixed on Celia and Herrick.

Storhmier studied him. Was that a false ring in Parnell's voice? Storhmier decided he was imagining things. "I wish I was a banker with no worries." He had the fleeting impression Parnell's jaw tightened.

"You just picked the wrong business," Parnell said jovially. His eyes never left the couple at the table. He saw Celia reach out and cover Herrick's hand. There must be a strong bond between them. To prevent his interest in them from being too apparent, he looked at Storhmier. "Quincy, isn't your loan almost due?"

"So that's why you came here," Storhmier said. "To dun me. I've got several months left yet."

"I know that," Parnell said hastily. Those little pig eyes had a calculating shrewdness in them. A few unwise words could arouse speculation.

Parnell changed the subject. "I see Herrick is cutting in on Lou's woman."

Storhmier snorted in disdain. "Lou's out of the running. From what I heard all farmers are just about broke."

"Does she know that?" Parnell asked smoothly.

"You can bet on it," Storhmier stated. "That one's got a sharp nose for money, but this time, her smell is dulled. Phil can't scrape up two dollars to rub together."

"He's sure trying to talk her into something," Parnell mused.

"He's barking up the wrong tree," Storhmier said. "Hell, he can't be sure he's got a job here for much longer."

"Ah," Parnell purred. "Things that bad, Quincy?"

"You know it," Storhmier replied. He managed a painful grin. "If worst comes to worst, you've got another business on your hands."

"Not me," Parnell said fervently. "It's your headache, Quincy."

"You enjoy that thought," Storhmier said sourly before he moved away.

Parnell's busy mind picked at the facts he had assembled from Storhmier. A slow exultation was spreading through him. He had something here, all he needed was to find the key.

He made his second drink last until Herrick got up and moved away from the table. Herrick walked outside, his face moody.

Parnell finished his drink. Things couldn't be working more in his favor. He had all the ingredients he needed, a money-hungry woman, a love-sick, desperate man. If he couldn't stir up a tasty brew out of that, his name wasn't Welles Parnell.

Parnell was careful not to let his haste show as he followed Herrick out of the door. Ah, he breathed in relief, as he saw Herrick leaning against a wall. Herrick was smoking a cigarette, his face harsh and drawn. Parnell knew that feeling. Here was a man driven by his thoughts to find a moment of solitude, to find a way out of his dilemma.

"Good evening, Phil," he said.

"What's good about it?" Herrick asked sullenly.

"I've got a proposition that might interest you," Parnell said.

"There's no way of you making any money out of me," Herrick said sourly.

"I'm thinking of you making that money, not me," Parnell said. "Are you interested?"

At Herrick's lack of response, Parnell said impatiently, "Will it cost you anything to find out about it?"

"I guess it couldn't," Herrick said reluctantly. "What's your proposition?"

"Be at the bank at ten o'clock in the morning," Parnell said before he walked away.

He could feel Herrick's eyes on him until he turned a corner. Would Herrick be there in the morning? He would, Parnell assured himself. Everything was working in his favor now.

CHAPTER SEVENTEEN

The frightened squawks of the chickens pulled Lou out of the house in a hurry. He jumped up from the breakfast table, overturning his coffee cup. He swore at the brown stain spreading across the table, but he had no time to do anything about it now. He knew what was happening. Some varmint was in the hen house.

He snatched his shotgun from its rack on the wall, pausing only long enough to thumb a shell into the chamber.

The terrified squawking had grown louder before Lou reached the hen house. He could hear the thuds of the hens' bodies as they flung themselves against the walls. They would dash themselves to pieces, if he didn't stop this.

Lou flung the door wide, and the chickens streamed out, their heads low, their wings beating frantically as they raced by Lou seeking safety.

Lou waited until the last one passed before he peered cautiously inside the structure. He jerked back in a hurry as he caught sight of the white striped black animal, standing over a dead hen. The skunk saw Lou, too, for it whirled, his tail going up in menacing threat.

Lou retreated hurriedly. A skunk was a bloodsucker, killing a chicken with a single bite through the neck, then sucking its victim's blood.

Lou was content to let a skunk go its way as long as that way didn't intrude on Lou's way. Now, it had happened. Lou had to get that skunk out of the hen house, but he was wise enough not to go in and try to drive him out. Nabor had been sprayed by a skunk a couple of years ago. People avoided Nabor a solid week after that.

Lou wanted to kill the skunk. Once the skunk had found its way into the hen house, it was likely it would return with members of its family. If that happened, Lou's whole flock of hens would be wiped out.

Lou fretted impatiently. Even if he could get a shot inside the hen house, he didn't want to blow holes in his building. No, he decided, the only thing he could do was to wait outside until the skunk made up its mind to leave.

The skunk finally emerged, stopping short just outside the door as its black, beady eyes caught sight of Lou. It stopped abruptly, humping its back. It looked as though it was going to whirl again and present that raised tail to Lou. Lou retreated hastily. He couldn't shoot the skunk while it was in front of his hen house.

The skunk was finally satisfied that Lou intended no interference. Its tail lowered, and it started moving slowly along the hen house.

Lou could swear there was a derisive attitude in the skunk's manner. The shotgun butt was up against his shoulder, and his finger was on the trigger. Just a few more steps and the skunk would be clear of the building.

Ah, Lou thought and pressed the trigger. There was no responding blast from the shell, and Lou remembered in dismay that the trigger of this gun had hung up like this the last time he had hunted birds. He had intended to have it fixed, but the bird season was over, and he had put the gun away and forgotten about it.

He kept the shotgun against his shoulder, swinging the muzzle with the skunk's progress. It probably wasn't more than a second, if that much, before the gun went off, but to Lou it seemed forever. A gun in this shape was damned dangerous; it could blow off a man's head.

The shell finally went off, and the butt slammed back into Lou's shoulder. He blew the skunk to hell. He grimaced as the pungent aroma drifted to him. It seemed as though a skunk was always ready to dump the contents of that musk bag.

Nalley came running around the corner of the house, his eyes wild. He saw Lou standing there, and some of the anxiety left him. "I heard a shot, Lou. What's the matter?"

Lou gestured at the small mangled form on the ground. "Skunk in my chicken house. I shot him."

"Whew," Nalley said. "I smell him now."

"This damned trigger is hanging up, Sam," Lou said. "I knew it was doing that when I put it away last fall. But I forgot all about it until I tried to use it just now."

"Is it empty now?" Nalley asked.

"Empty," Lou assured him. He broke the shotgun as proof and handed it to Nalley.

Nalley pulled out the empty shell and dropped it onto the ground.

He reassembled the gun and pulled the trigger. There was a definite pause before it clicked.

"Better get this fixed before you use it again," Nalley said judiciously.

"I'm taking it in this morning," Lou replied. He might not use it again until next fall when the ducks and geese began to fly, but if he didn't get it fixed now, he'd wind up forgetting about it again.

"I've got to get a shovel and bury that skunk," Lou said.

Nalley dubiously shook his head. "Won't stop the smell."

Lou was well aware of that. Even after the animal was buried, the smell could linger for days. But burying was the first step toward getting rid of it.

Lou came back from the barn with a shovel. He dug as far away as he could get from the skunk and still reach it by tossing shovelfuls of dirt upon the body. He stopped only after he had a little mound on the ground. Nalley was right. The smell seemed as powerful as it had before.

Lou put away the shovel and rejoined Nalley. "I didn't let the chickens out the first thing after I got up this morning." He shrugged. "I guess it wouldn't have done any good. That skunk got in through some hole. I'll have to find and plug it up later."

"I don't mind a skunk as long as he stays where he belongs." Nalley grinned. "And that's never too close to me."

Lou nodded agreement. "Join you in a minute, Sam." He hurried into the kitchen and finished his cold piece of toast. He wished he hadn't spilled that cup of coffee. He went into the bedroom to dig out the five hundred dollars from its hiding place.

He came out and laid his plowshare on the floor of the buggy. Nalley had carried the shotgun out with him, and it leaned up against the seat.

Nalley sucked on a knuckle. He held up the hand for inspection. The knuckle was skinned and bloody. "I had one hell of a time getting that damned share off," he grumbled. "One of the nuts rusted on me. I worked on it until dark last night and started on it again early this morning."

Lou shook his head in sympathy. He knew how exasperating a stubborn nut and bolt could be. "Why didn't you come over after me?"

"A dozen men couldn't have done any better," Nalley said crossly. "I soaked that bolt in kerosene last night." He grimaced at an unpleasant memory. "Remind me to get some more. I had to drain one of the lamps."

Lou nodded. How well he remembered where Nalley's drum of kerosene had gone.

"I didn't think even that was going to do any good," Nalley said and clucked to the mare. "That's when I busted this knuckle. Maude said she heard me swearing clear up to the house."

Lou grinned. "Did she bawl you out?"

"No, she came down and just looked at me," Nalley replied. "That was enough. I was ready to give up when I thought I'd give it one more try. You know that damned nut gave?" Nalley had a wondering note in his voice. "Lou, do you suppose the devil has anything to do with rusty nuts?"

Lou chuckled. "Could be. Quit stewing over it. We lost an hour or so. We're not in that big a hurry."

"I really can't blame the devil for this," Nalley said reflectively. "It's my own fault. I should have oiled that plow before I put it away. Something came up, and I promised myself I'd get back to it. You know how it goes. One thing after another kept turning up until I forgot about it."

Lou touched the shotgun. How well he knew. Any little delayed chore grew teeth, and the more it was delayed, the longer the teeth grew. If he hadn't remembered that shotgun trigger hanging up, he could have blown his head off, by trying to find out what was wrong with the gun.

"I want to go to the bank first, Sam. I've got Edmonds' money in my pocket. I woke up twenty times, thinking of that money. Every time I wanted to get up and check and see if anybody had found it." Lou said that lightly, but he was more than half serious.

Nalley treated the subject with the same seriousness. "Enough to worry any man. If it'd been me, I would've held the money in one hand and gun in the other." His eyes were intent on the road.

"Lou, the womenfolk and me talked a lot about what you're doing." His voice roughened. "Hell, it's giving us new hope. No, more than that, it's a new life."

"Oh, for God's sake," Lou said wearily. "I thought that was all settled last night. Are you going to harp on it all the way to town?"

Nalley slapped Lou on the thigh. "I won't say anything more about it."

Lou felt just fine. The old Sam Nalley was back, and that was what Lou wanted. Sure, he needed Nalley's physical strength, but most of all he needed his belief. With those two things back of him Lou didn't see how he could miss.

"After we go to the bank," Lou said, "we'll drop off the shares at the blacksmith, stop and leave this gun at Harley's, then stop at the feed store." At Nalley's inquiring look he explained, "I've got to find out where I can get seed wheat. I doubt if Miller has any, but he should know where I can get it. Sam," he said plaintively, "there's so much to put together, and I'm so damned ignorant."

"Know exactly how you feel," Nalley said. "How do you think I'd feel, if I wasn't with you?"

"It's going to work, Sam," Lou said positively. He wouldn't let it turn out any other way.

"We'll work our butts off," Nalley promised.

All the rest of the way to town, Nalley hummed a tuneless song. That's what belief does for a man, Lou thought. Without hope a man is dead.

Nalley started to pull up before the bank, and Lou said abruptly, "Keep on going, Sam. I just saw Herrick go into the bank."

Lou laughed ruefully as Nalley's eyebrows rose. "I'd just as soon not run into him again. The last time I did, I got the hell knocked out of me."

"It wouldn't happen this time," Nalley growled, but he slapped the reins on the mare's rump to keep her moving. "Where do you want to stop first? The blacksmith's?"

Lou appreciated Nalley's attitude. Nalley understood why he wanted to avoid Herrick. Lou wished he could also avoid seeing Celia again, but he couldn't. It hit him with a sudden clarity he didn't want to see her again, but it would be shameful for him to duck an obligation he had built himself. No, he thought, I'll see her some other time when Nalley isn't around. It was a form of running, but Lou couldn't help it.

Nalley pulled up before Sanders' blacksmith shop. Lou followed him into the building. The little room was hot and cluttered. Hy Sanders was at his forge, beating lustily at a piece of metal and didn't see Lou and Nalley come in.

Lou picked his way through the litter in the shop. Scraps of metal, old and new, were everywhere. He didn't see how Sanders found anything in this place.

Sanders was a big, burly man, stripped to the waist. Sweat ran down that thick torso, and huge muscles rippled with every movement of his arm.

Lou touched Sanders on the shoulder. Nothing ever startled Sanders, even when he was in the midst of absorbing work.

He turned his head and grinned at Lou. "Don't give me any rush job," he warned. "I'm snowed under. I've got four horses to shoe, plus some repairs."

"I didn't think people had any money," Lou commented.

"I didn't either," Sanders admitted. "I guess this was work that just had to be done." He looked at the plowshares Lou and Nalley carried. "This rush will pass, then I'll sit on my ass, waiting for more work." He sighed and added, "Ain't it always that way?" His face brightened. "But I won't be holding you up. You've got plenty of time to get your plowing done."

"Not this time," Lou answered. "We're putting in wheat. The plowing has to be done now." He half expected to see derision on Sanders' face.

"Might be a good idea," Sanders said reflectively. "I know wheat plowing has to be done earlier, but I can't put you ahead this time. It'll have to be tomorrow at the best, Lou. Late tomorrow. I'll stay here until I get it done. Say about eight o'clock."

Lou shook his head at Nalley's unhappy look. "That'll do just fine, Hy. I'll pick them up."

"It's always that way," Nalley said disgustedly as he and Lou walked out. "Man wants to get to work, and something always stops him."

"Another day won't kill us, Sam."

"I guess you're right, Lou," Nalley said. "Want to go to the bank now?"

"I'll stop at Harley's first," Lou decided. He wasn't sure whether or not Herrick had come out of the bank.

Harley's gunshop was opposite the bank, and Nalley stopped before the building. "Want me to come in with you?" he asked.

"I'd appreciate you keeping an eye open for Herrick," Lou said. "I won't be more than a few minutes."

Harley was a badly crippled man, but his fingers were clever at tinkering with a gun. He got up as Lou entered and limped to the counter.

"Harley, this trigger is hanging up," Lou said as he handed Harley the gun.

Harley pulled the trigger several times, listening to the delayed click. "No big job," he said. "I'll have it turned out in no time."

"No rush, Harley. I've got to come into town tomorrow night. Will you be open around eight o'clock? Hy can't have my plowshares ready until then," he explained.

"I'll make it a point to be open," Harley said and smiled. "Good thing you're having this done before you use it again. Coulda got your head blown off."

Harley didn't know how right he was. It had almost happened to Lou this morning.

Lou went back out and started to climb into the buggy. "Herrick just came out," Nalley said, stopping him. "I saw him go down the street."

"Then let's get rid of this money, Sam. It gets heavier in my pocket every minute I carry it around."

"I can bet," Nalley said fervently. He climbed down from the buggy and walked across the street.

They entered the bank, and Mills was in his cage. It was a relief not to have to see Parnell. Lou had an idle curiosity as to what Herrick was doing in the bank, but he didn't ask. That was none of his business.

Mills's eyes were unforgiving. "It won't do you any good. Mr. Parnell isn't in."

Mills's manner amused Lou. "I came in to see you, Charley." He pulled the bills out of his pocket, took the passbook out of his shirt pocket and shoved them toward Mills. "For deposit, Charley."

Mills counted the money, made an entry in the passbook, and handed it back to Lou. Lou looked at the new figure before he tucked the book back into his pocket. It was just a little under a thousand dollars. That was a hell of a lot of money; it should take him where he wanted to go. But not if you go throwing it around, an inner voice cautioned him. Lou chuckled. That voice should know Lou never had a reckless hand with money.

Lou patted his shirt pocket as he rejoined Nalley. "We're in business, Sam. Now, let's go see Miller and find out what we can do about that seed."

Nalley drove to the other end of town and stopped before Miller's feed store.

Miller sat dozing in a tilted-back chair when Lou and Nalley walked in. Lou leaned his weight on the tipped-up edge of the chair, forcing it down against the floor. The front legs hit the floor with a loud bang.

Miller came up out of the chair, his eyes wild. He was a short, rotund man and usually good-humored. He wasn't at the moment. "You could've broken my neck," he hollered.

"I'm sorry, Ed," Lou pacified. "I just couldn't resist it. I guess you won't want to do any business with me now."

Miller tried to keep his face straight, but a grin pulled at his lip corners. He couldn't keep it from breaking out. "Damn you, Lou Manard. I thought my building was coming down around me. Did you say business? Hell, I'm desperate enough to do business with the devil."

Nalley looked at Lou. "How do you tell the difference between them?"

Miller laughed. "When I first came up out of that chair, I thought I was looking at the devil himself."

"A couple of smart asses," Lou said and grinned. "Business really that bad, Ed?"

"How could it be otherwise?" Miller replied. "I don't know what people are going to do."

Lou remembered Arnold's words. "They'll get by." That sounded cold and unfeeling, and he added, "In some way."

"That 'some way' is going to take skin off of them," Miller observed. "Did you come in here just horsing around, Lou, or did you have something definite in mind?"

"Definite, Ed," Lou answered. "How much is seed wheat going to cost me? I want only red Turkey wheat."

Miller's head was cocked to one side in interest. "Going to that, Lou?"

"Both of us. Sam and I just got tired of being wiped out by drought one year and hoppers the next."

"You might be smart at that," Miller said judiciously. "How much are you planning to put in?"

Lou took a deep breath and plunged. "All we can get in. Between Sam and me, I'd say two hundred acres. More if we can get at it."

Miller whistled. "You're going for broke."

Lou grimaced. That might be the softest way of putting it. "How much is that seed going to cost?"

"I don't know," Miller replied. "I haven't got any red Turkey seed. I tried last year to stock a little, but no one was interested."

Dismay swept across Nalley's face, and Lou knew what Nalley was thinking. Here was another insurmountable obstacle in their road.

"But you can get some, can't you, Ed?"

"I sure can," Miller said with enthusiasm. "Take me about a week. Let's see. At a bushel and a peck of seed to an acre, you'll need—" He broke off and reached for a piece of paper and pencil. He did some rapid figuring. "You'll need about two hundred and fifty bushels. I think you could safely figure on it costing you about a quarter a bushel."

Lou gagged at the amount of cash that would take. But he'd never learned any way of making money without expending some.

"Go ahead and order it, Ed," Lou said decisively. "You think it'll be in, in about a week?"

"For that big an order, I'd go to hell and carry it out on my back," Miller said happily. "It'll be here."

Lou nodded and started to walk out. He remembered something and stopped. "Ed, you got any oats? I need about four sacks. Going to have to feed the horses, if they're going to work hard."

Miller shook his head. "I couldn't scrape up a sackful, Lou. Stricker cleaned me out. He came in here a week ago and took every oat I had. I guess the grasshoppers scared him, too. Maybe he'd let you have a few sacks."

"I'll check with him," Lou said and walked out with Nalley.

Nalley's face hadn't lightened, and Lou said, "Don't be thinking of another delay. We've got a hell of a lot of work to get done before we need any seed."

Nalley's face cleared, and he said, "I've got into a sorry habit of thinking low, Lou."

"Easy to fall into," Lou said easily. "Things are going just fine, Sam."

Nalley climbed into the buggy and lifted the reins. "I guess I'm just itching to get at it."

"Both of us are," Lou said quietly. He was silent a moment, thinking of the trip he had to make into town tomorrow night. He didn't want Nalley along, for he was determined to talk to Celia and get that over with.

"Sam, I'll come in tomorrow evening and pick up the shares and my shotgun. Harley said it'd be ready, too." He was silent as he pondered how he should make the trip. He guessed he'd come in the wagon. He would need the space, if Stricker had those oats. He could check with him today and make sure, but he didn't want to take the time.

"Sure you don't want me to come along?" Nalley asked.

"Positive," Lou replied.

CHAPTER EIGHTEEN

Mills opened Parnell's office door. "Mr. Herrick's here, sir."

Parnell glowered at Mills. The old fool is getting senile. He could see that Herrick was here.

"Charley, go out and get a couple of cups of coffee. And I don't want to be disturbed for a while."

Parnell waited until Mills closed the door. "Sit down," he invited. "You're prompt."

"You said ten o'clock," Herrick said indifferently. He couldn't see why Parnell wanted to talk to him.

Herrick sat down. "Now what's this proposition you said might interest me?" He sounded completely bored.

Parnell stood and walked to the door. He opened it and looked out into the other room.

"Charley's gone after the coffee," Parnell said.

Herrick showed some surprise. "You ordered him to, didn't you?"

Parnell sat down and smiled. "I just wanted to be sure he wasn't around. Charley's got big ears." He laced his fingers across his paunch and leaned back in his chair. "How would you like to earn two thousand dollars?"

Herrick's eyes burned with interest. "That's killing money, mister. Who do you want killed?"

Parnell's eyes shone with pleasure. He had debated offering Herrick only a thousand dollars, then decided on the larger sum. He wanted to be sure he captured Herrick's interest. All he had to do was to look at Herrick to know he had succeeded.

Parnell kept studying Herrick, and Herrick squirmed uncomfortably.

"Get on with it," Herrick said impatiently.

Parnell held up a pudgy hand. "Don't rush things," he said mildly. "I want you to know everything about this proposition. You know that Storhmier is about to close?"

"I wouldn't be surprised," Herrick said irritably.

"I hold a big loan on his place," Parnell purred. "With the way business is he can't possibly meet his note."

"Will you tell me what you have in mind?" Herrick asked impatiently.

"I just wanted you to know that your job won't last long. When Storhmier closes, what will be left for you? I don't want to see you stranded." Parnell rotated his thumbs, letting the tension build up in Herrick.

"I'll give you that two thousand dollars, and you can ride out of town with no questions asked," Parnell said.

Herrick's eyes narrowed. "Nobody gives money away like that without a definite reason. What's behind all this?" he growled.

Parnell lifted his hands and let them fall. "Nothing! Can't a man do a charitable thing without having to say why?" He chuckled ruefully. "I guess I might as well tell you everything. I saw the way you feel about Celia. I also know that Manard is after the same woman." He leaned toward Herrick, his face guileless. "I also saw you knock Lou Manard down the other day right out in front of the bank. It wasn't hard to see that you don't have any love for him."

The intensity of Herrick's stare made Parnell nervous. "Maybe you never heard this before, but Manard knocked me down one night." His face twisted malevolently at the memory. "The law refused to do anything about it. But a man doesn't forget something like that."

Herrick's eyes never wavered. "I heard something about it." It wasn't possible, but it sounded as though Parnell was willing to pay for wiping out an indignity.

"So you see I have every reason to see Manard hurt. I think taking Celia away from him would do that. Two thousand dollars is a lot of money, but it's worth that to me."

Parnell waited anxiously, hoping to see some comprehension in Herrick's cold, implacable face. "You understand, don't you?" he begged.

He wanted to cry with relief as he saw a slow grin steal over Herrick's face. The damned fool believed him.

"I'd have to think it over," Herrick said slowly. "And I'll have to talk to Celia about this."

Parnell's assurance returned and with it his contempt. Herrick was a weak man; he couldn't make a move without first asking a woman's permission.

"I thought you'd want to leave right away," Parnell murmured, trying to keep the disappointment out of his voice.

"Oh, I do," Herrick said quickly. "But there's several things I have to see to. I'd need to buy a couple of horses." He looked suddenly woeful. "How can I do that? I'm broke."

Parnell's gesture swept away the minor obstacle. "How much would you need?"

"I'd say two hundred dollars," Herrick replied. "I should be able to buy good horses for that."

Parnell's exultation rose. Herrick had made up his mind; he was going to take the offer. "That's no big problem," he said, smiling.

He pulled his wallet from his pocket and counted out ten twenty-dollar bills. "The rest is yours when you want it," he said.

Herrick looked up at the ceiling, and Parnell didn't interrupt his mental figuring.

"I wouldn't be able to leave until tomorrow night," Herrick said. He swept away the disappointment in Parnell's face by saying, "I've got some obligations to attend to. A man can't just pull up and leave on a moment's notice."

Parnell swallowed hard. He had Herrick in his hand, and he didn't want to lose him. "I guess not," he admitted.

Herrick stood and pocketed the bills. "Good," he said briskly. "I'll be here at eight tomorrow evening."

Parnell wanted to scream, but he held it back. Herrick would be back here at the time he said. The thought of eighteen hundred dollars would more than see to that.

"That'll be just fine," Parnell said with false heartiness. "I'll be waiting for you."

He walked to the front door with Herrick just as Mills came in carrying the coffee.

"We don't need that coffee now, Charley," Parnell said. "We finished our business quicker than I expected." His eyes gleamed as he watched Herrick walk down the street. Another day wouldn't make any significant difference. He had all the time he needed.

2

Herrick threw back his head and laughed as he walked away from the bank. Just wait until he told Celia about this.

Celia was just coming down the stairs as Herrick entered Storhmier's. Her eyes were too feverishly bright, and Herrick thought, she's spent a restless night.

"You're up early, aren't you?" he greeted her.

"I didn't sleep very well, Phil."

"Sit down," Herrick invited. "I want to talk to you."

"What makes you so chipper this morning?" she asked crossly.

Herrick reached out and captured one of her hands. "Remember what I said about taking you to New Orleans? I can now."

He grinned at her astonishment. "You don't believe it." He released her hand and pulled the bills from his pocket. "Count it," he said.

Her eyes widened as she did so. "Two hundred dollars," she whispered. "Where did you get this?" She shrugged and temper flashed in her eyes. "I don't see where this makes any difference. Two hundred dollars won't take us far."

Herrick picked up the money and stuffed it back into his pocket. "You'll understand when you hear the rest of it. There's eighteen hundred dollars more coming."

How he enjoyed the incredulity sweeping across her face. He stopped her outburst by saying, "Just listen."

Rapidly, he told her of his talk with Parnell.

"He hates Lou that much?" Celia asked.

"Maybe he does," Herrick answered. "But whoever heard of a banker paying that kind of money to soothe his pride?" His eyes danced, and he seemed in complete charge. "The fool didn't think I could see the real reason behind his offer."

Celia's eyes were wide. "What's his real reason?"

"That's not hard to see," Herrick said contemptuously. "He's been ruined just like everybody else. Now he's short in his books, and it must be close to auditing time. He gives me two thousand dollars, then reports a much bigger robbery." He shook his head impatiently. Celia wasn't understanding this at all. "A robbery will get him in the clear. The robber will be blamed instead of Parnell."

She understood now, for her face paled. "But you'd be blamed." She raised a hand to her throat. "You're not even considering taking his money!"

"The hell I'm not," he said savagely. "I've already taken two hundred dollars. Do you think I'm going to pass up the rest?"

He breathed hard, and his eyes were filled with a fierce light. "I'm going to take every cent he's got in the bank."

Herrick couldn't believe his eyes. Celia was shaking her head, and her lips were trembling.

"Don't tell me you're turning this opportunity down," Herrick snapped. "Parnell's going to let me into that bank tomorrow night. I'll never have a better chance."

My God, she was sobbing now. "Phil, he'll have somebody waiting for you when you come out. They'd shoot you down. I couldn't stand that."

His grin returned. "Don't you think I haven't considered that? There won't be anybody waiting for me. Parnell has to let me get away before he announces his robbery."

Tears kept welling up into her eyes, and in a moment she would be bawling.

"Stop it," he said sharply. No one had come into the room yet, but they could at any moment. "Damn it, Celia, this is the opportunity I've waited for all my life. He's going to let me into the bank tomorrow night to collect my eighteen hundred dollars." He grinned wolfishly. "That fat banker will be surprised, won't he?"

"No, Phil," she whimpered. "I won't let you do it."

Herrick's laughter was a short, mirthless bark. "You won't let me? Celia, you can't stop me." He looked at her speculatively. "I jumped at this because of you, Celia. I'm going ahead with or without you. You've been whimpering how much you wanted to leave this miserable town. I want you to go with me. But you can stay. It's your decision."

Celia closed her eyes and shuddered. When she opened them, there was a sickness in them. "Phil, it could be so dangerous."

Ah, Herrick thought, she is weakening. "Not much, Celia," he said soothingly. "You could be of help to me."

"What could I do?" she gasped.

"I'm going to buy two horses today," he replied. "I want you to hold them for me until I come out of the bank."

She looked paler than ever, and he thought she was going to faint.

"For God's sake, Celia. Do you think I'd put you in any real danger? You'll have the horses ready in that alley a half block from the bank. In a few minutes, we'll be on our way. Don't look like that. We'll be long gone before Parnell announces he has been robbed."

"You'd kill him?" she whispered.

"I'll do whatever I have to do," he said grimly. "Make up your mind, Celia."

Her face was ghastly, and she couldn't speak.

Herrick stood and shook his head. "You're passing up the chance to live the way you want to. I'm not."

"Phil," she gasped. "Wait a minute." She struggled with her words. "I'll do whatever you want me to do."

CHAPTER NINETEEN

Lou left home an hour earlier than necessary to accomplish his errands. It would give him ample time to talk to Celia. God, how he dreaded that. He knew now what he was going to tell her, but he just didn't know how to say it. Bluntly, he guessed, was the only way. He would withdraw all the glowing promises he made her, and he knew how scorn would fill her eyes. Maybe that was what he dreaded most.

He thought of what he would say all the way into town, then shut his mind to any further thinking along this line. It wasn't going to do any good to stew about it. Maybe Celia would cut him off after a few words and save him the agony of further explanation.

I'll try Stricker first for my oats, he decided as he drove into town. He knew what he was doing; he was only putting off the inevitable.

He drove into the stable's runway, as Stricker came out of his office.

"What can I do for you, Lou?"

"Cal, Miller said you cleaned him out of oats. I need four sacks bad. Can you spare any?"

"Just might be able to," Stricker said. "Ordinarily, I wouldn't consider it, but I sold a couple of horses this morning."

"Didn't think you'd find a buyer with that much cash money right now," Lou said as he climbed down.

Stricker chuckled. "Business comes from the damnedest sources. Last man I'd figure to be in the market for two horses. Phil Herrick bought them," he announced casually.

He grinned at Lou's expression. "Thought that'd hit you."

Lou tried to keep his face blank, though thoughts were churning in his mind. Herrick didn't need two horses unless he was taking somebody with him. Celia, Lou wondered? It could be. The thought brought him no pain at all. Dear Lord, Lou would be grateful if it was so.

"Do I get those oats, Cal?"

"Give me a hand with them. Some of them are still sacked."

Lou helped Stricker carry the oats back to the wagon. "You don't know how grateful I am, Cal," Lou said as he paid for the oats.

"Don't mention it, Lou."

Lou got back into the wagon and raised a hand in acknowledgment.

All his dread was gone now. He had the feeling things were working in his favor. He had to believe it wasn't going to be hard to talk to Celia now.

Lou drove toward Storhmier's. A half block from the place, he saw Celia walking down the street.

"Hold up, Celia," he said, drawing Molly to a stop. He sprang from the wagon and hurried toward her. It would be easier to talk to her out here than in Storhmier's with curious eyes watching him.

"You took your time coming back," she said sullenly.

"You know what's happened, Celia," Lou said. "Things changed a lot since I last saw you." He grinned painfully. It was still going to be hard to tell her.

He swallowed and went on, "The grasshoppers just about wiped me out, Celia. I wasn't lying when I made all those glowing promises. Oh, I'll get by, but it's going to be a strain." He shook his head. "I wish it could be different, but it isn't."

Lou stared in amazement. Celia was laughing scornfully.

She controlled her mirth and said, "The last thing I thought I'd ever see, an honorable man. Trying to explain why he can't keep his promises to a lady."

She shook her head in wonder. "Maybe it's best it's happened this way, Lou. I told you it wouldn't work for either of us, but you wouldn't listen."

He couldn't believe it, but she was giving him his release. She wanted to be free of him.

"I'm sorry, Celia," he said soberly.

"Don't be," she said. "I'm not." She looked into his face, and her eyes had a brightness he hadn't noticed before. "Don't give me another thought." She reached out a hand as though she wanted to touch him but quickly withdrew it before she made contact.

"I'm going to be just fine," she said huskily. "I'm leaving this sorry town, Lou."

So Herrick had bought the horse for her. For just a moment, Lou knew a faint sorrow for what might have been, then it was quickly gone, leaving not the slightest trace.

"If it's what you want, I'm glad," he said steadily. "All the luck in the world, Celia."

She almost touched him again. "I always said you were sweet, Lou," she said huskily.

Lou wondered if she, too, remembered a shining moment between them.

"Don't worry about my luck," she said almost fiercely. "I found out you have to give it a little help." She bobbed her head and moved away from him.

Lou stared after her until she entered Storhmier's. My God, he couldn't believe it. He was free, without any nagging little teeth of conscience gnawing at him.

Lou wanted to shout at the top of his voice. He grinned as a thought struck him. This was a switch, a man being so happy after he'd been turned down.

He looked again at Storhmier's door before he climbed back into his wagon. "Good luck, Celia," he said aloud and meant it.

"Come on, Molly," he said, slapping the reins across the mare's rump. "Let's get our errands done." Lou wanted to get home as fast as he could. He had something to tell the Nalleys, particularly Maude. His face sobered at a distressing thought. How would Maude accept this change? Would she look at him with scornful eyes, or would she lacerate him with a merciless tongue? Lou was suddenly scared as he'd never been in his life.

"No," he said passionately. The denial lacked conviction. No matter how badly Maude treated him, he had earned it.

Lou got the worry off of his face as he pulled up before the blacksmith shop. He sure didn't want Sanders asking questions.

He walked into the building. Sanders had removed his leather apron. He stood at the tub of water, sloshing handfuls of water onto his chest.

"If you knew how I busted my ass to get your work done," Sanders said. "Other things took me longer than I expected. I just finished your shares not fifteen minutes ago."

He looked at Lou and added, "Hell, I thought that'd make you happy."

"It does," Lou said hastily. He didn't want Sanders to have any knowledge of the misery that was tearing his guts apart. It would remain there until he talked to Maude. Or get worse, he thought.

He picked up one of the shares and ran a thumb gingerly across the cutting edge. "Good job."

"Good, hell," Sanders retorted. "You can shave with it."

Lou paid Sanders the small amount he asked for the work. This was another of the small drains a man couldn't figure on, but they would keep cropping up.

"Thanks, Hy," he said as he picked up the two shares.

"Anytime," Sanders answered.

Lou nodded and walked out of the shop. He placed the shares in the wagon bed. One more thing to do, and he was through in town. That was going to be a dreary ride going home. All the way there, he would be sweating about how Maude would take his words.

Lou changed his mind about driving to Harley's gunshop. It was only a half block away. It wouldn't be worth the driving.

CHAPTER TWENTY

Herrick swung down and handed his reins to Celia. "You know what to do?" he asked.

The small alley seemed to suddenly close in on Celia, and she shivered. "You won't be gone long, Phil?" she implored.

For a moment, temper rose in his face, but he managed to keep his voice even. "Good God, Celia. We've gone over everything. You're not scared, are you?"

"A little," she confessed. She swallowed hard. "It's only because you'll be gone."

"Not far," he said impatiently. "I'll be back before you know it." He pulled out his watch and looked at it. "Five minutes to eight, Celia." His eyes were critical as he looked up at her. She seemed so pale. Was she going all to pieces on him?

"Get ahold of yourself," he said coldly. "Nothing's going to happen."

He pressed her knee and smiled. "This is the beginning of everything we've wanted, Celia. You'll see." He turned and strode toward the mouth of the alley.

"Be careful," Celia said in a low voice. Herrick didn't answer, but he lifted a hand in response.

Herrick patted the flour sack folded into an inner pocket. It should hold all the money this hick-town bank had. He briefly touched the pistol butt under the skirt of his coat. Nothing could go wrong. He had planned too carefully.

He came briskly down the street, passing the bank, noticing a light was on. Good, he thought. Parnell is waiting for me.

Herrick walked down to the end of the block, turned and came back, repassing the bank. Nothing was amiss that he could see. It must be very close to eight, now.

Herrick turned and retraced his steps. He stopped before the door, looked all about him, then tapped on the door. He considered knocking again, this time louder, but Parnell was waiting near the door, for it opened quickly.

Parnell reached out and drew Herrick inside. Herrick could feel the tremor in his hand. He's scared out of his wits, Herrick thought with cold amusement. Wait until he realizes what's happening. Then he'll really be scared.

"Am I late, Mr. Parnell?" he asked.

"Right on the minute," Parnell said. He tried to laugh, and it came out weak. "For a while there I was afraid you'd decided not to take advantage of my offer."

"I did some thinking on it," Herrick confessed. "Then I couldn't pass it up. Celia and I are ready to leave, Mr. Parnell. You don't realize what you're doing for us."

"That's all right," Parnell said jocularly. "It's worth the satisfaction it'll bring me."

"I hope it brings you everything you want," Herrick said smoothly. A hurried glance around the room located the safe for him. He didn't know how he was going to make Parnell open it. Then he remembered what he said to Celia. He'd do whatever he had to do.

Parnell visibly brightened. "I mustn't keep you, if you're ready to leave." Exultation was a savory taste in his mouth. This was going exactly as he planned.

Parnell walked toward the safe and dropped onto his knees before it. "Wait until I get the rest of your money," he said. He looked up at Herrick and smiled. "You didn't expect me to carry that much money around with me?"

"No, sir," Herrick said gravely. He was glad Parnell didn't look at him longer. Surely, the naked satisfaction would be apparent in his eyes.

Herrick moved a noiseless step until he stood just behind Parnell. In his wildest hopes, he couldn't have believed this was going to be this easy.

Herrick pulled the gun from his waistband and waited tensely for Parnell to finish opening the safe.

The door swung open, and Parnell reached into the safe.

"I'll take care of that for you," Herrick said harshly.

He struck savagely with the gun barrel as Parnell turned a startled face toward him. The barrel caught Parnell across the top of his head. Parnell tried to rear up, but the strength wasn't in him. He groaned hollowly and spilled forward on his face.

Herrick shoved him out of the way with a boot toe. He pulled the sack from his pocket and crouched before the safe. His hands trembled, and his eyes glistened as he saw the neatly stacked packets of money. He worked with feverish speed as he stuffed the packets into his sack. Hadn't he told Celia he was going to get back in a hurry?

2

Lou noticed a light was on in the bank as he entered Harley's shop. Probably old Charley working late, he thought. With a boss like Welles Parnell, Mills should be used to late hours.

Harley limped to the counter and picked up Lou's shotgun. "As good as new," he said. "The trigger won't hang up any more."

"Good," Lou replied. He broke the gun and saw that its chamber was empty.

"You didn't think I'd have a loaded gun around the shop, did you?" Harley asked.

Lou grinned. "Just making sure." He snapped the gun together and turned, not wanting to point even an empty gun anywhere near Harley.

Lou froze as he stared out of the window.

"What's going on?" Harley asked.

"I wish to God I knew," Lou replied. His suspicion was growing until he could think of nothing else. He had seen Herrick go into the bank yesterday morning, and here he was back again after banking hours. That was more than enough basis for suspicion.

Harley peered across the street. "I don't see a damned thing."

"Not now," Lou said in a low voice. "Have you got a shell that'll fit this shotgun, Harley?"

Harley handed him a shell, and Lou slipped it into his gun. He grinned bleakly at the impatience forming in Harley's face. "There might be a robbery going on in the bank right now. Damn it, Harley. I've got to make sure. I've got money in that bank." He didn't add that was money he desperately needed.

It seemed an eternity while Lou waited. Would Herrick come out of this entrance, or was there another door? The indecision wracked Lou. Harley's strained breathing didn't help.

This was the card Lou had been dealt, and he had to play it. All he could do was to wait here and see what happened.

"Somebody blew out the lamp," Lou said in a low voice, as he saw the light extinguished. "Ah, he's coming out now."

For a moment, Herrick was framed in the doorway. He looked both ways before he stepped out. He carried a white sack, and it showed up distinctively against his dark clothing. There was something furtive about the figure. The speed with which Herrick went down the street confirmed Lou's impression.

"Don't come out, Harley," Lou warned and stepped hastily out of the door. He crossed under the metal awning that shadowed the walk and stepped out into the street.

"Hold it right there, Herrick," he called. The shotgun was cradled against his hip.

Herrick threw a shocked angry look at Lou and reacted faster than Lou expected. He stopped and whirled, and his other hand came into view. Lou caught the flash of light on something metallic.

Lou struggled to bring up the shotgun, realizing he had made a bad mistake. The shotgun should have been at his shoulder and ready before he gave Herrick that order.

Lou didn't see the muzzle flash of Herrick's gun nor hear the heavy report, but something smashed into his shoulder with brutal force. It knocked him stumbling backward until a post of the metal awning stopped him. He hung there, grateful for its support, for without it he would have gone down.

His left arm was practically useless, and sweat beaded his face as he fought to raise the shotgun. He got it high enough for the left hand to give the gun a little support. It seemed that the effort had taken forever, and Lou's vision was darkening.

He sobbed in harsh, wracking breaths as he forced his eyes to focus on Herrick. The indistinct figure was almost at the mouth of the alley.

Lou pulled the shotgun's trigger, and the roar of the heavy blast rocked back and forth across the street. The recoil of the heavy weapon was powerful enough to tear the gun out of his hands.

He heard a man's scream, rising shrilly before it snapped off in midnote.

Had he hit Herrick? Lou could no longer see, and he wished he knew.

The effort to remain erect was too great, and Lou just let go. Now, his ears were playing him tricks, for he could swear he could hear a woman's scream. The ground rose swiftly to meet him. Lou didn't know when he crashed against it.

CHAPTER TWENTY-ONE

Trying to get his eyes open was like swimming upward through thick, clinging mud. No matter how hard he tried, Lou couldn't seem to break through. Maybe he would never be able to open his eyes again. He lay there, thinking about it. Is this what death is like? If so, it wasn't frightening. He didn't hurt, and he was comfortable. But he was so damned weary.

No, he thought violently. He wouldn't allow himself to be dead. That amused him, and he wanted to chuckle. That made him sound like a big, important man, so badly needed that he wouldn't be allowed to die.

He heard voices, and they seemed to come from a long way off. Memory had an irritating way of scratching at a man when it wanted to return. Like a damn dog scratching at a door, wanting to get in, Lou thought.

He lay there, listening to those voices, trying to place them. They sounded so familiar. Now, he was beginning to hurt. It started in his left shoulder, and the pain was spreading and getting fierce. He wanted to yell against it.

"Are you sure, Doc, that he's going to be all right?" a distant voice asked.

Lou almost had that voice, but it slipped away before he could fully grasp it.

"He's as strong as a horse," a testy voice answered. "I put him under sedation after I dressed his wound. He should be coming to any time now. Lou always was luckier than he has any right to be. The bullet didn't break any bones or tear up any muscles too bad. In a few weeks he won't even know it happened."

Lou knew that cranky old voice. That could be nobody else but Doc Logan. All this could mean only one thing. He wasn't dead. The excitement of the idea popped Lou's eyes open.

Things were a little blurred, but he could see better than he hoped for. But something puzzled him. It was broad daylight, and he was certain he had been shot at night.

He tried to sit up, and a wave of pain shattered him. His mouth flew open, and a yelp of pain escaped before he could stop it.

Dr. Logan and Briner rushed into the small back room. "Easy, easy," Logan said testily. A hand pushed Lou back and held him there. "It took me long enough to fix that wound and get it dressed. Do you want to rip it open?"

"It hurts like hell, Doc," Lou complained.

"I can give you something for that. But only if you lie still for a while."

Lou was perfectly content to follow instructions. He lay back, and memory flooded in like an incoming tide. He was back before the bank, and Herrick was shooting at him. Lou recalled shooting back at Herrick, but after that everything was a blank.

"How'd I get here?" he asked weakly.

Logan was fussing around in a cabinet, and Briner answered. His face was grave with concern as he looked down at Lou. "Harley ran and got help. Four people carried you here. Most excitement Russell has known in a coon's age." Briner sighed. "If you know how long I've been sitting out there, waiting to talk to you."

Logan came back, and Briner said aggrievedly, "Doc, are you going to let me talk to him now?"

"Depends on how he feels," Logan grunted. He held out a pill and a glass of water to Lou. "Take this," he ordered. "It'll ease the pain."

The water washed down the pill, and Logan said, "It'll start taking hold in a minute. Do you want to talk to the sheriff?"

"I've got to," Lou said excitedly. "I've got to let him know what happened."

"I think he already knows," Logan said dryly. "But go ahead."

Lou started to raise up again, but Logan's firm hand held him in place. "I can stop your talking in a hurry, if you don't behave yourself," Logan said.

Lou managed a weak grin. He didn't want that. There were some things he needed to know.

"Will, did I hit Herrick?"

"You blew him to pieces," Briner said soberly.

"He was robbing the bank?" Lou held his breath for fear the answer would be no.

"He sure as hell was," Briner said emphatically. "About every dollar the bank had was in the sack Herrick carried." He eyed Lou speculatively. "You stopped him good. Maybe you're thinking of getting my job."

"I wouldn't have it as a gift," Lou said fervently. "My part in it was just a lucky accident. I was in Harley's, picking up my shotgun when I saw Herrick go into the bank. It struck me funny because it was after banking hours. When he came out he was carrying a sack. I just thought it ought to be investigated. I yelled at him to stop. Instead, he shot me."

Briner gave him a crusty grin. "You sure as hell thought right."

"Poor Charley," Lou said and shook his head.

Briner looked surprised. "Why do you say that? Mills had nothing to do with this."

It was Lou's turn to look puzzled. "Somebody let Herrick in. I thought it was Charley."

Briner snorted. "Hell, no. It was Welles. Herrick hit him over the head with his gun barrel. Welles was still out when I found him. When he came to, he was full of words, but none of them fit very well. The safe door was standing open. Welles had to be the one who opened the safe. I think there was some kind of a deal between him and Herrick. Anyway, I'm impounding the money until the bank examiners come in. I've got a hunch they're going to find a big shortage in Welles' books. I thought he was going to faint when I told him that." Briner shook his head. "I didn't care much for Welles for a lot of reasons, but I never figured him to be crooked."

"I've got money in that bank," Lou said in alarm.

Briner gave Lou a sour grin. "I don't think you have much need to worry. You saved this community from losing most of its money. I think you'll be given special consideration. I'm not saying the Bank Association is going to reward you for what you did, but they might. They've done it in other cases."

Lou shook his head. "Just the money I have is all that interests me."

"You can forget about losing it," Briner said.

"I'm glad Charley wasn't involved," Lou said. He was silent a long moment. "Things sure work out funny, don't they, Will?"

"They sure do," Briner asserted.

Lou remembered one other thing he wanted to ask about. "I thought I heard a woman scream before I blacked out. My imagination, I guess."

"No imagination, Lou. It was Celia."

At Lou's stunned look, he nodded and went on. "She was bending over Herrick when I arrived. There were two horses in the alley. She denies she knew anything about them, but Herrick bought those horses from Stricker. I locked Celia up. I know she's involved in this with Herrick." He looked pityingly at Lou. "I'm sorry."

"No need to be," Lou said. "Everything was dead between us. What's going to happen to her?"

"I'd say nothing much, Lou. It's her word against circumstantial evidence. She's a pretty woman." Briner shook his head in resignation. "If she sticks to her story, I'm afraid a judge will look at her and let her go."

Poor Celia, Lou thought. He remembered their last meeting and the shine in her eyes. She was so positive everything was going to be all right for her, and instead everything had come crashing down around her head. Lou examined his innermost feelings. He felt pity for her but nothing more.

Briner stood and said, "Lou, Doc says you're going to be just fine. Oh, you'll be laid up for three or four weeks but nothing more. You were lucky, Lou."

Lou nodded slowly. All the luck was with him and against Herrick and Celia. Poor Celia, he thought again. It was odd, but just in this short time her face was growing hazy. Tomorrow, he would hardly be able to remember her at all.

"I'll look in on you again," Briner said and started toward the door. He stopped, and his voice was husky. "I don't have to tell you how much we all owe you."

Lou made an unwise movement with his left hand, trying to dismiss Briner's words. The movement cost him pain. "It was nothing," he said.

Briner looked at him quizzically. "Everybody knows better than that, Lou," he said softly.

Logan left the room with Briner, and Lou listened to voices coming from the outer room. There had to be another person in there with Logan, for that wasn't Briner's voice.

"How do you ever expect him to recover?" Logan asked irascibly, "if you don't give him a minute's peace?"

"Briner talked to him," the new voice yelled angrily. "You're not going to tell me I can't see my son?"

Lou grinned. That was Doyle's voice. Logan might as well give in.

Logan followed Doyle into the room. "Not more than a couple of minutes," he said stiffly.

Doyle advanced to Lou's bedside and looked down at him. "I always heard a smart man doesn't get himself all shot up. Thought I taught you that."

Lou grinned broadly. Doyle was attempting to be funny, but there was a peculiar shakiness in his voice. "Something like this happens every time I don't follow your advice, Pa."

"You gonna be all right, Lou? Briner said you were, and even the old fusspot here," Doyle jerked his head toward Logan, "admitted you're going to be all right, even with all his bumbling."

Lou controlled his impulse to laugh. When these two old pieces of flint got together, sparks were bound to fly. "I'm going to be fine, Pa."

Doyle reached down and squeezed Lou's good hand. "I did some worrying when I first heard about it," he said roughly.

Lou blinked to keep the moisture out of his eyes. This was about as close to sentiment as Doyle would ever permit himself to go.

"Lou, I been thinking about your advice. I ain't going to use it right now. Don't frown at me," he barked. "I'm going to tuck it away in my head. I'm not going to forget about it. If the grass comes back at all, I figure I can get through. Hell, Lou!" His eyes begged Lou for understanding. "Raising cattle is all I know. I can't change until I'm driven up against a wall."

"Sure, Pa," Lou said gently. Maybe some tough instinct was guiding Doyle Manard, and maybe he'd fall flat on his face. But it was Doyle's road, and he had to travel it.

Lou's understanding cleared Doyle's face. "Don't think I won't be watching you like a hungry wolf. If you show me how I can make more money your way, I'm not too stupid to ignore it."

Lou returned the pressure of his father's hand. "It's going to work out just fine for both of us, Pa." Personally, he thought that one of these days he would see Doyle switch to wheat, but he felt no bitterness that Doyle preferred to wait. He felt real good about what Doyle said. Doyle had another way to go, if he chose it, or necessity drove him to it.

"Are you going to stand around yakking all morning?" Logan snapped.

Doyle grinned at Lou. "Mean old cuss, ain't he? I'll see you soon, Lou."

"You can bet on that," Lou replied.

He listened to the wrangling between the two as they left the room. Those two came out of the same cantankerous mold.

Contentment spread through him. He guessed a man had to go through a certain amount of strain before things straightened out for him.

"Oh God," he heard Logan yell in the outer office. "Not more. You people act as though you just heard of a revival being held here, and you're rushing to attend."

Lou turned his head toward the door. That couldn't be Doyle Logan was yelling at. It had to be somebody else.

The door flew open, and Maude literally ran into the room. Nalley followed his daughter, Maude's face was pale, showing evidence of too much stress.

"Lou," she cried and rushed up to him.

He thought she was going to throw herself upon him, then she must have reconsidered, for she stopped and drew back a step. The pallor of her cheeks was rapidly being covered by a tide of crimson.

"Oh, Lou," she whispered. "I was so scared." Her eyes kept straying from his face. "Riley heard the news and hurried out from town to let us know what happened. I thought Pa would never get here."

Lou smiled. "No need for all that hurry. I guess Doc told you what happened."

Maude nodded weakly. "Briner filled us in, too." She looked as though she would break into tears. "Lou, I'm so sorry about Celia."

"Ah, you know about that, too," Lou murmured. "Maude, look at me. There was nothing left between Celia and me. That's been dying for some time now. I was just too dumb to see it. I'm sorry for Celia, too. But she dug whatever hole she's in. It just doesn't matter any more."

Maude stood as though transfixed. Her lips were slightly parted, and a shine was beginning to appear in her eyes. Nalley stood behind her, grinning like an idiot.

"Maude," Lou said plaintively, "do you understand what I'm trying to say?"

Good Lord! The radiance lighting her face awed Lou. What in the world ever made him think she was on the plain side.

Maude hadn't moved an inch toward him, and that scared Lou. Maybe he had acquired wisdom a little too late.

"Maude," he said woefully, "I'm a damn fool."

Maude's face was thoughtful, but her eyes crinkled from some inner mirth. "I guess there's a streak of that in every man, Lou. But some of them manage to outgrow it. Maybe you're one of those."

Lou's eyes burned, and his throat was tight. It wasn't possible, but she was forgiving him for everything.

"Maude," he asked huskily, "would you help me be one of those lucky ones?"

Tears filled her eyes, but there was a glorious shine in them. "Oh, Lou," she said.

Nalley picked the wrong time to interfere. "How are you doing, boy?" he asked. "Doc says you managed to stir up a little excitement."

Lou didn't want to talk to Nalley, but he said, "Guess I did. It's going to change our plans some." He went on, sweeping away the worry that sprang into Nalley's eyes. "I won't be able to keep up my end of the plowing for a while. But it doesn't make any difference," he hurried to say before Nalley's worry could spread. "You can hire some help until I recover. You won't have any trouble finding somebody who needs work."

Nalley looked stupefied, and Lou said, "Don't start worrying about that, either. We can handle it. Nothing's going to stop us now." He remembered something important and said, "Sam, you'll have to keep checking with Miller until that seed gets in. Then you'll have to get it by yourself."

The happiness on Nalley's face was dazzling. "That won't be a problem."

Lou thought everything had been covered, but Nalley still stood here. Lou wished he could get Nalley and Logan out of the room. Maude was about to tell him something important when Nalley interrupted. Good God, did he have to get up and throw them out of here?

"Dr. Logan," Maude said. "Lou is going to need care while he's mending, isn't he?" She said it without a doubt in her voice.

"He sure will," Logan replied. "He's going to need good care for a while. That shoulder will make him pretty helpless."

"Can he be moved?" Maude asked.

Logan's face was sober, though his lip corners kept twitching. "Any special place in mind, Maude?"

Maude's blush extended from her neckline to the roots of her hair, but her eyes didn't waver before Logan's probing look.

"Why, yes," she said steadily. "Out at our place. Ma and I will be around to take care of anything he needs."

Nalley bobbed his head in complete agreement.

Logan stroked his chin while Lou held his breath. Damn it, Doc, he pleaded silently. Say yes, because I'm going anyway. I'll get out there, even if I have to walk. I've got to find out what Maude was going to tell me.

"I don't see why not," Logan finally conceded. "If we make a pallet in the wagon and take it slow, I don't think the move will hurt him. But let me warn you. He'll be a miserable patient. He's a stubborn man and does anything he pleases."

Maude's serenity didn't dim. "You know, Doctor, I think I can do something about that."

Lou smiled at her. That was exactly what he wanted to hear. She will too, he thought. Somehow, it didn't alarm him at all.